CW01082823

PROLOGUE

The nighttime is a special place for a special kind of person. But what if you're not just a person? There have been many religions, stories, and fairy tales that have been passed down from generation to generation, but what do we really understand about vampires, witches, and werewolves? What about aliens? We have no idea, as a society we have no irrefutable proof that ghosts do not exist. What if I told you that these beings are not always what you think they are? People always forget that Frankenstein was the scientist that brought him to life, not the monster.

At the end of the story, they banished the poor stupid monstrosity to oblivion, simply because he looked different. To be fair, just because he was made from human parts, doesn't mean that he was human. His empathy, blissful ignorance, and compassion made him a target because he was a freak. The real monsters were the people that set his home and his life on fire. Real monsters in any horror film, always stem from that one asshole who thinks their opinion is the most right out of everyone else's, just because they are the loudest and the biggest bully. What if I told you that all of the stories about "monsters" were true?

The thing they got wrong is that they have feelings, and problems just like humans do. The biggest flaw with the human race is their confidence and egos. Humans put a man on the moon, therefore, they are the supreme race of the universe. There can be no other intelligent life in the universe, especially if you can't see them, right? Well, the problem with that is humans have no way of really understanding the world around them let alone the universe. Humans think they have it all figured out, but vampires do not sparkle in the sun.

Some mystical beings are more complicated than just being vampires and witches. The problem is if humans can't use their primitive senses to observe something, or they can't capture it on their cell phones and put it on YouTube, it doesn't exist. The world is still flat, according to some village idiots, there is a whole tribe of fools who believe that. One of them even built a rocket to prove the Earth was flat, then died when he tried to pilot it. Let's just say, he wasn't a rocket scientist.

Here's the thing, just because social media says something's not real, doesn't mean that it's not. Queen Victoria and the monster society she belongs to would disagree. They have to keep their identities secret and if they go public, they will be hunted down like dogs, or Frankenstein's monster. Being burned alive is no death fit for a queen. She lives in an old, scary, haunted castle on the top of a big hill, just at the edge of town. It is hidden from outsiders by magic, and what a magical place it is! Queen Victoria no longer has village idiots to rule over, so she has simply been living in her castle with her dog, Bandit, and her one loyal subject, who will never leave her side, Wilson. Is she a witch, vampire, or something else?

The inside of the castle is just as old and creepy as you would expect. It is pitch black, the only light source is a flashing of lightning in the background and gas-lit candles along the huge corridors. Some classical music plays and the lights slowly come up. It is still very dim. A beautiful woman, dressed in all red, holds a small dog and sits on a throne. There is a side table next to her, and a red glass of wine sits on it, she picks up the wine and chugs it. She lets out a sigh of relief.

Victoria says, "I really needed that, who wouldn't after the day I've had? It's such a struggle living like this, eternally isolated, doomed." She turns to the dog.

"At least I have you to suffer with me," she says in a baby voice, "Isn't that right Bandit? Yes, you are the goodest boy!"

She speaks calmly, in her normal voice, "I've learned that not all who wander are lost. Some of those lost sheep will never find their way. Some of those sheep should be pushed off a cliff, and some of them wander off. Good riddance." She says. "We are all sheep in one way or another. Our shepherd is a devious asshole who enjoys being omnipotent but is also apathetic to his herd. As if there is a god, ha! There's no all-powerful being watching our suffering and getting off to it, the truth is far worse than that. We are utterly alone, forced here to live every day and never die, no matter how much we beg for death. When will I ever find something to give my life meaning? Besides Bandit, of course." she sighs deeply.

The lightning outside flashes, and there's a glimpse of something behind her. There's a body lying on the floor, in the shadows, and there is a puddle of blood under the body. The lights go out, darkness floods the air. It gets cold, icy. Everything fades to nothing, as all time, space, and matter eventually do.

CHAPTER 01

Victoria is in a graveyard, the moon is very bright in the background. She walks around staring off into the distance longingly, sighing loudly and using very dramatic, over-the-top gestures. She walks through the misty haze, floating. She looks down at her dog. She looks up and spots a couple sitting near a grave. They are making out and talking indistinctly. She slowly and silently approaches them from behind the gravestone. She peaks her eyes over the stone, they don't see her. She looks around suspiciously, leaps over the gravestone, and eats the girl first. The unknown male shrieks and does a backflip off the ground to get away from her. Victoria's back is to him.

He is frozen in fear. He sees her holding his girlfriend, she rears her head up and bites her neck with a loud crunch. The blood pours out of her, it drenches the ground, pooling at Victoria's feet. Victoria drops her lifeless body with a loud thud. It seems to happen in slow motion for the unknown male, he sees all of the happy memories with her flash before his eyes. He is promptly brought back, in a quick snap, as her body lands with a thud.

He screams, "NO!"

Victoria turns around, quickly, her eyes are glowing red, and she is snarling as she approaches him. The guy screams in horror, she laughs evilly. She gasps for air and gets near him. She wipes her mouth, now drenched with blood, on her sleeve.

"Don't worry honey, you're next, I thought you'd be smart enough to run away, stupid boy," she howled at the unknown male, who had just witnessed this horrific murder. He tries to run, but he feels like no matter how fast he runs his feet go nowhere. She has trapped him in an invisible bubble. He is stopped in his tracks by a force he has never felt before. With a small wave of her hand, she releases him from the bubble.

He falls. She cackles so loudly that it echoes. She is playing with him, a game of cat and mouse, invigorated with the power she has displayed. He is terrified. He starts hyperventilating. It makes her hungrier when he begs for his life. She approaches him with the hunger for his blood in her eyes. He plays dead for a minute but when she gets within range, he swings his leg around and begins doing capoeira moves. He misses her head wildly, her reflexes are inhuman. She looks confused and laughs.

"You look fucking ridiculous right now, I just want you to know that, is this really how you want to die? Hey, now that I've seen your face, you're kind of cute. Are you down for a quick drive to pound town? I mean, before I ruthlessly and brutally murdered you, like I did to your hoe. What was her name by the way?" Victoria laughs, as she taunts him, the blood from his girlfriend still dripping down her chin.

"Get away from me, you crazy ass bitch," the man says as he continues trying to use his capoeira to kick her, but she dodges it every time. She laughs and taunts him, louder and more aggressively.

"Oh sweetie, this is just sad, I want to suck another fluid out of your body, but if you're not down for that, I'm not going to force anything that's not consensual. I'm not that kind of woman. What's your name?" she says condescendingly.

He stops kicking at her for a second in disbelief. "Well, I didn't expect you to. I wasn't the one who was acting all threatening and bloodthirsty, just for the record. My name is Xander, why do you want to know, so you can scream my name later, when you touch yourself, thinking about how you murdered me and Sofie? By the way, you look really familiar." Xander cries, gasping for air.

"Sofie is a cute name for a poodle, can't really say that you have good taste, but she tasted all right, I guess. I've had better. When you put it that way, it makes me sound kind of pathetic. I'm not even really hungry now. You've made me lose my appetite, douche. You know what, instead of killing you and ending the suffering, I'm going to give you something way worse." Victoria says, she stares, as she floats away from him.

Lightning strikes, and she appears right behind him. Lightning flashes again. She is about to bite his neck from behind. He feels her hot, tingly breath on him. It makes the hair on his neck stand on end. He gets goosebumps, and everything goes black.

Xander wakes up on the floor of Victoria's castle. It is still very dark. He looks around very confused. The floor is cold. With every move, it creaks under his weight. He stands, hesitantly, not sure if someone is nearby. He smells a faint odor of sandalwood and roses. It's intoxicating, he has a series of violent flashbacks. He sees Sofie getting murdered in front of him. He cries for her and pounds his fists on the floor and slams down on the ground. He sits on the floor on all fours. He is crying so hard he can hear the tears hitting the cold ground.

Xander collects himself, stands up, dusts himself off, and spots the only light source in the room - a candle on the wall near him. He picks it up and begins looking around, trying to find his bearings. He shines the light near his face and Victoria appears behind him. He turns around quickly, and she disappears. He turns around again, she appears in front of him and says, "Boo!" He screams in terror and drops the candle on the floor. Victoria picks it up and has a very annoyed face.

"Be careful, you almost lit this gorgeous hardwood floor on fire, idiot!" she screams, in his face, startling him.

"Why is it so dark in here anyway? Don't you have any modern amenities, like lights, a stove, things most people have in their creepy castles?" he wines.

She rolls her eyes, so hard they practically roll out of her head and makes an annoyed sigh. She replies, "I mean, I do, there's a switch on the wall right behind you, but I like the dark and I wanted to be creepy when you woke up. I thought it would be more entertaining. I haven't had anyone here for a while and I get lonely. I can only pleasure myself so many times before it gets sore." Victoria says.

Xander takes the candle out of her hand. Her vision goes blurry for a second, she breathes deeply and collects herself. When he touched her hand, she felt something she hadn't felt in an awfully long time, and she didn't know what to do about it.

All kinds of scenarios flash before her eyes, he turns around and looks for a light switch on the wall. Victoria snaps out of it, he lights up the entranceway and looks around in awe. Victoria is seen with her head in her hand. She sighs, then looks up at him. He sees her true face. He jumps and yells.

"I'm not going to hurt you, calm down jumpy man, you've already got the gift of eternal life, why are you scared?" she said, in a calm, soothing voice.

"What is this place and how did I get here?" he inquired as he looked around, trying to take everything in.

He noticed that there were many knick-knacks on the walls, little trinkets that all had cobwebs from the obvious age of the castle. Xander got a sense of dread, a sinking feeling in the pit of his stomach. He knew something was not right about what she was saying. What did she mean by giving him the gift of eternal life? He didn't feel any different from before he arrived in the castle. He wasn't sure what was going to happen next. He was a prisoner who had been overpowered by this fancy, ball gown-wearing queen. How was he supposed to fight back if she tried to attack him? There was also a faint smell in the air, sandalwood and roses. She approached him with caution, her eyes were black as night.

"I mean, isn't it obvious, why I brought you here?" she said with a slight hint of sarcasm in her voice.

"It isn't, what do you want from me? Why have you brought me here, how could I be of any use to you? You're a queen in a castle. I work in a pizza parlor, in town, for minimum wage." he replied, with anticipation for her answer.

"Why had she brought him here," Xander thought, "the truth seemed obvious, yet not so much. Is she a cannibal? Is she going to make me her sex slave, oh no, what if she can hear my thoughts?"

He felt his stomach sink again.

"I thought I explained this, I just wanted a friend and you begged me not to kill you after I ate that VD-riddled slag that you were getting hot-and-heavy with. You should thank me, you could do better - just saying - and her breath, woof! I mean, I'm one thousand years old and I brush the corpses out of my gums. It's not that hard." Victoria says.

Xander is bewildered by the things she is saying. He can't stop thinking about Sofie and what Victoria did to her. The flashbacks return. He sees the life drain out of her eyes, he snaps back to this reality. He tries to speak, but his mouth is dry. His throat feels sore. He coughs, trying to clear his throat. He gathers himself enough to reply to her, struggling to form his thoughts. His mind is racing, still picturing his lost love.

"What... what do you mean the gift of eternal life?" he croaks, hoarsely.

"Oh my God, you are so thick, just figure it out! Look in a mirror or something."

Victoria is visibly annoyed, her eyes turn bright red. She stamps her feet and collects herself. She pulls a small bell from her cloak and rings it, she yells, "Wilson, get over here now. Why do I even keep him? He probably got into the playboys that I had stashed in the attic again." She mutters.
A small, weasely, voice is heard behind Xander. He turns around and sees a small creature with a puss-filled scab for a face. He jumps and moves out of the way. Wilson walks up to Victoria and tries to hug her. She nudges him with her foot and looks at him with disgust.

"Yes, mistress?" he squeaks pathetically.

"Take him to his bedchamber. We want to make our guest feel welcome, so get him anything he needs," she says, rubbing her temples.

Victoria kicks Wilson in the ass and laughs. He looks back. He begins to laugh. Victoria threatens him with her backhand. He chirps softly, he hightails out of the room as fast as he can, and he yells back at her, "Right away, mistress."

Xander hesitates for a second, he looks at Victoria, seeking reassurance. She waves her hands, annoyed, and he follows Wilson. He looks around, this hallway has many axes and battle armor on the wall, and the hallway seems to never end. There is a large bookshelf, he looks at the books. One stands out to him. It is called "Being Human." He sees another book, it reads "Twilight." Other books say, "Interview with a Vampire", "The Witches", "Dracula", and "Lord of the Rings".

"She's really into fantasy and horror books." Xander thought to himself.

He feels a tugging on his pants. He looks down and sees Wilson pulling on his pant leg. He kicks him and Wilson hits the wall, Xander cups his hands over his mouth in shock, he immediately feels bad. He runs to him and Wilson whimpers pathetically. Xander grabs his arm and helps Wilson to his feet. Wilson leans in to give Xander a kiss. He pushes him away in disgust.

Wilson dusts himself off then he continues walking towards his room. Xander continues following him. He looks back and forth.
There are so many things on the walls and in displays along the walls that his eyes are dancing. He is enticed and amazed by all of the items, so ancient, yet somehow still shiny. The ceilings are so high, he's not sure if he can see the top of them. The castle gets bigger and has no ending. Finally, they reach his room, Victoria is waiting for them, she is sitting on a fancy lounge chair, with a glass of red wine. There is just something Xander finds mystifying about her, mesmerizing. He is bewitched and sedated by her perfume, roses, and sandalwood. He sees the world through a pink haze. "Could I be in love? How could I, that's ridiculous, I just met her, and she murdered Sofie," he thinks to himself. He just can't shake her off of him, it feels like they are connected somehow. Now, she is a part of him. Wilson reaches for Xander's hand, it is equally disgusting and moist, Xander quickly swats his hand away. Wilson whimpers and breathes with effort and wheezes, loudly.

"It's almost morning, you better get in your room before the sun comes up or you're going to be in big trouble," Victoria says, with a slight giggle in her voice.

"What do you mean big trouble, like you're going to hurt me, rape me, drink my blood? What are you, some kind of witch, or vampire, like in Twilight or something?" he asks, remembering all of her vampire and fantasy books in the bookshelf.

"There are so many amazing books, movies, shows, and media on vampires and Twilight is the one you referenced, really?" she scoffs, and spits out her wine in disbelief.

"I love Twilight! It's so deep and filled with passion. Besides, you have it on your bookshelf. Did you read it? The books are so much better than the movies." Xander says confidently.

"I thought it was boring and the actors were more dead onscreen than the chick I ate last night. Have I made a mistake with you? I read it, and used the pages when I ran out of toilet paper."

Victoria can barely contain her laughter. She slowly approaches him. He starts doing his capoeira moves and kicking at her.

She continues, "What the hell is that, are you having a seizure or something? Did they do that in Twilight?"

He is insulted, and he stops kicking for a minute.

"It's Capoeira, an ancient form of dance fighting. I am a master, and I will kick your head off if you get any closer." Xander shouts in frustration.

She laughs so hard she snorts; she can barely gather herself enough to choke out a few words. "Ok, you can stay, you are hilarious! Wilson, take him upstairs. It could be worse; you could be a fan of Kanye or something," Victoria laughs.

Xander looks insulted and scoffs before replying under his breath, "I love Kanye, his last album was a masterpiece."

Victoria hears this, stops laughing, and hisses in his face, then disappears. Xander covers his eyes and with a flash of light, she's gone. He breathes heavily, stops his breathing for a second, and looks down, freaked out. Wilson is there breathing very loudly and with a lot of effort. He shivers in disgust and takes a step away from him.

"I have got to get out of here," Xander says breathlessly.

Wilson laughs and says, "If the mistress has her way, you'll never get out, you probably won't even be able to find the front door. Stupid newbie." Xander looks around, he looks directly behind him, there is a huge wooden door, he points to it, he giggles.

"Is that it?" Xander says with a slight matter-of-fact grin.

Wilson looks around and stomps the ground, in frustration, he speaks with a wheeze, "Well, yeah, but I wouldn't recommend leaving right now. You'll die. You should trust me. Follow me, I'll show you to your room."

He gestures for Xander to follow, and with some hesitation, he follows him. He stops.

Xander says, confused, "Wait, if she is some kind of ancient witch lady, how come she is so current with modern media?"

Wilson is shocked by his ignorance. He stops in his tracks and gives him a confused and angry look. Xander can barely see him in the dim lighting of the hallway, all he can make out are his glowing eyes, but he still sees them squinting at him.

Then Wilson squeaks, "She's got a lot of money, I bought her a computer, TV, and pretty much everything we have here, we even have pretty good Wi-Fi."

Xander pulls out his phone and looks down at it. The light from his cellphone illuminates his face. He has giant fangs sticking out from his two front teeth, his ears are much pointier than they were before, and his eyes glow red. Wilson smiles and realizes that the ritual to turn him worked better than expected. "How can he not believe or be so ignorant?" thought Wilson.

"Oh shit, what is the wifi password? I need to check my email." Xander exclaimed. There is a loud hissing noise and a puff of red smoke, the smell of sandalwood and roses fills the air. Victoria appears.

She yells with a booming voice, "Goddammit Wilson, I asked you to do one thing, show him to his room. How hard is that? Fuck it, I'll do it, just follow me, idiots."

She gestures to them, frustrated, she looks up and notices that the ritual she did to turn him is working. She smiles to herself and tries to contain her joy, she squeals, Xander looks up from his phone for the first time since Victoria appeared, he quickly looks back down and goes back to not paying any attention.

He says defiantly, "No, I'm not going to do what you want me to do."

Victoria's eyes turn red. She hisses so loudly that the sound reverberates in Xander's chest and head. He faints from the force of the sound. Everything goes black. He feels himself hit the floor and he loses consciousness. Then there is only silence and blackness. Everything else fades away.

CHAPTER 02

Xander wakes up in a coffin. He starts banging on it loudly. He is gasping for air and frantically trying to get out. The wooden walls of the coffin are already small and begin closing in on him. He claws at his neck, trying to make a hole to breathe from. His heart is pounding so loud that he can't even hear his screams over his own heartbeat. There is the sound of a large, creaky, wooden door opening. There is a slight movement at the bottom of the coffin. A light peaks out of a tiny pinhole. Xander is terrified. Is it another ghoul minion, bigger and scarier than Wilson? Who knows what kind of horrors are waiting outside the coffin for him? All the thoughts of how he will escape from a giant foe flood his mind.

"I could find something heavy and whack him on the head, giving me just enough time to distract him and escape," he whispers in his head, readying himself for whatever could be about to attack him.

He sees the visions of Sofie being ripped apart by Victoria. He cries, it was a distant memory. He can barely see her face, covered in blood and lifeless, falling to the ground, with no regard. How can he not see her face? She was the love of his life. Or was she?

The coffin door flies open. Xander's fists are raised, ready to kill anything that may harm him. He looks around and looks down, in shock and horror at how upset he was. It's just Wilson, standing with a silver platter in his hand. It has a goblet of red wine and a charcuterie plate for him. A smile barely peeks out from under Wilson's puss-filled scabs. Xander smiles back for a minute. Without any warning, he feels his fight or flight instincts kick in, his legs carry him by force. Xander shoves Wilson out of the way, so hard that his tiny, misshapen body imprints a dent in the wall as he collides with it. Wilson gives out a pathetic squeak as he hits the wall, going through the drywall, then the ground, with a thud.

Xander runs down the hall, faster than he's ever felt his legs carry him. He feels like he's flying. All of his senses are heightened. He feels invincible, and strong, but also confused. He looks down and notices that his feet aren't touching the ground. He stops and looks around, gasping for air.

Xander sees the front entrance. He's almost free, he can taste it. All of a sudden, there is a pink cloud misting in his eyes, making it hard for him to see or focus. The familiar smell... Queen Victoria is nearby. No matter how hard he fights for his freedom, he's being held back like a magnet. He turns around and there is a dining room with candles on a long, pretty table. He stops to look at it and Victoria appears in a puff of pink smoke. She gestures at the table, she smiles.

She says with a matter-of-fact grin, "How was your nap? I hope you slept well, I have made a feast for you, I'm sure you're hungry."

Xander approaches the table, hesitantly, he sits down and looks around. Queen Victoria sits, and Wilson pushes her chair in for her. She waves him off. He leaves through a two-way door and the smell from the kitchen behind the door wafts in. Xander can see the smells, a grayish cloud fills his head with visions of the most exquisite prime rib he's ever tasted. He is very intrigued by the meal she has prepared for him. He can't leave, he feels his freedom mere feet away and yet he is compelled by an unknown force to sit down.

His legs force him down in the chair. He sees a table set for two, something off in the distance catches his attention - something he can't quite place, somehow familiar, but also foreign to him. Then, he catches another whiff of some delicious-smelling beef or some kind of meat. He can't place it, but the smell of dinner is somehow even more intoxicating than Queen Victoria.

"What happened? How did I end up in that coffin? And what is that intoxicating beef that is cooking in the kitchen?" Xander blurts out, trying to gather himself and struggling to focus on saying simple words.

"Well, you fainted, I was worried you were going to have another one of your weird dancing, martial arts seizures. I put you to bed, so you wouldn't hurt yourself," she states, boldly.

"Why are you doing this to me? Also, what is that smell? It's amazing! Did Wilson cook for us tonight?" He says frantically, still having trouble focusing.

"Why thank you! If Wilson didn't cook, why would I keep him? A good servant cooks, cleans, and is obedient to a fault, that's what I've always said. Don't worry, I haven't done anything to you, trust me, you're my guest," Victoria says.

Wilson knocks the door open. He is holding a platter with a pitcher of red wine, a fileted steak, a gravy boat with a red gravy, and a plate of mashed potatoes. Wilson walks slowly around the table. He wheezes and struggles to move. Victoria gets frustrated and starts tapping her toe loudly and giving him an evil glare. Finally, he finishes serving Victoria. He begins walking towards Xander, walking with a limp and wheezing, loudly. Wilson serves him with a very shaky and disgusting-looking hand. Xander makes a face in disgust, but the smell of the food is so enticing he can hardly contain his excitement.

It seems like Wilson is going to spill at any moment, he is very uneasy on his feet. Xander and Victoria watch intently. They hold their breath in anticipation, then, Wilson finishes serving him, and they breathe a sigh of relief. Wilson wanders off, he has a nasty brown stench cloud of dog feces and rotten flesh around him, Xander gags as he limps off. Victoria picks up her fork and knife and she cuts her meat, ever so delicately.

Xander can hardly wait. He hears something tell him to be patient and not to take a bite until the queen has eaten first. She takes her time bringing the fork to her mouth.

All the while, Xander is holding his breath in excitement. He can't wait to destroy this meal like he has never devoured anything in his life. She puts the meat in her mouth, chews very slowly, giggles, and dances slightly in her chair. She swallows, then she gestures to Xander. He hears her tell him to enjoy and begin eating. He takes a bite and scarfs it down at lightning speed. He finishes, chugs his wine, wipes his mouth, and sighs loudly. His eyes flash a red color, then he looks up at Victoria and he pats his stomach, feeling satisfied.

"Wow, that was the most delicious thing I've ever tasted in my life. What did you put in it?" he asks.

Queen Victoria replies, "Well, you know a little of this, a little of that... I'm glad you liked it so much, maybe there is hope for you. I got bored only drinking one thing, so sometimes I like to switch it up. Would you like to join me in the garden for a stroll on the grounds? I promise you that I'm not that bad if you give me a chance and I won't hurt you unless that's something you're into."

She rings her bell, then she shouts for Wilson as she rings her bell frantically.

Xander hears labored breathing behind him. He turns and moves his arm out of the way in disgust, as Wilson walks over to Victoria. She pats his head and whispers into his ear. He nods and walks to Xander. He holds out his hand, but Xander swats it.

"Mistress would like to invite you to try on some clothes that she's made for you. Please follow me." Wilson chokes out, between wheezes.

"Ok fine, I'm just not going to hold your hand," Xander says, repulsed.

Wilson throws his hand to his side in frustration, then he gestures for Xander to follow him.

Xander throws his napkin on the table and gets up from the table. He follows him through the same hallway he went down last night. Xander looks around the mansion in awe. Everything is shinier and more beautiful all of a sudden.

Everything around him has an aura, its unique smell, and taste. All his senses are so heightened. He can barely contain himself, feeling so overwhelmed by all the sensory overload, but also drunk from it. Or was it the wine? Wilson opens a door where there is a big wardrobe, a mirror, and a box for him to stand on. Wilson opens the wardrobe and hands him a three-piece suit. Xander looks at it skeptically, then starts taking off his shirt. He notices Wilson staring at him, breathing heavily, and gestures for him to leave. He stands there shirtless, admiring himself in the mirror. He hears Wilson's breathing behind him. He looks down. Wilson is touching himself.

Xander gets down from the box and kicks him across the room. Xander stands back up on the box and continues admiring himself in the mirror. He puts the suit on one piece at a time. He sees himself, now more muscular and glowy than he has ever seen himself. "Truly a sight to admire, man I'm so gorgeous, how could any woman resist me? I never knew I was gay, at least gay for myself. Maybe I'll find a lady that will be gay for me." he thinks.

The memories of Sofie are so far away. She only died yesterday yet, for some reason Queen Victoria is never far from his thoughts. He can barely see his dead girlfriend's face. "What was her name again?" he thought, then the most wonderful smell in the universe, the smell of a queen. He closes his eyes and sees her face in his mind.

"Queen Victoria," he mutters, breathlessly. He feels a strong pull in his chest, then time slows and stops. Everything goes black.

CHAPTER 03

Xander opens his eyes and finds himself outside in the backyard. Queen Victoria is standing there looking magnificent. The perfume she wears is just divine and dances in his nostrils. Queen Victoria opens a black lace umbrella. She is wearing a fabulous red ball gown, a hat with a small lace face shield on the top, black lace gloves, and a train that goes on for days.

"How can anyone be as beautiful as you are tonight? The way your face glows in the moonlight makes me reevaluate my existence on this planet. I never knew there was such beauty in the universe," Xander says smoothly.

Victoria giggles and blushes, and her eyes flash pink. Then Xander offers her his arm and they walk holding hands. Xander and Victoria are in a large cemetery. It is attached to her castle, glistening in the moonlight in the background. Bandit and Wilson are following close behind.

Victoria speaks with purpose, softer than normal. "You see, we all come from the same collective being, energy, god, universal essence, whatever you want to call it. Religion is all just a bunch of hooey that people use to control each other. I call the collective Anu, the ether, the in-between, it's where beings like you and I are forced to dwell."

He can't concentrate, he's so enthralled with her intoxicating scent and her beauty. He is barely able to form a sentence.

He manages to choke out, "Sssso... so, Anu, what is that like a religion, a secret god that gives you the power of some kind of eternal life? I don't believe in any of that. The Earth existed billions of years ago, we are born, we're here for about eighty years, we die, and then the Earth continues. There's no all-seeing thunder god in the sky who controls our impulses. There's no eternal life of superpowers, I think you've been isolated in your tower for too long."

Victoria says, in disbelief "But, you are a... didn't you look at yourself, the vanity I set up for you?"

"See, that's a perfect example! I could see myself in the mirror. Isn't that part of ancient lore, that you don't appear in mirrors?" he asks, in protest

She speaks matter-of-factly, "No, here's the thing, old mirrors were made with silver, so we have no reflection, it's an adverse reaction. That's why ancient beings such as I didn't appear in them. Now they're made with a cheaper glass mixture. So, we have a reflection, I googled it."

Xander puts his hand gently on her face, cupping it and rubbing it with his thumb. "You're cute," he says, smiling.

He leans close to her face, he acts as if he is going to kiss her, but then he strokes her chin and leans his face away from her. She gasps. He turns around, leaving her to recover, vocally, from her excitement.

"But then again, if I did have some kind of crazy superpowers, I could use them to get what I've always wanted, a career in stand-up comedy. I have a lot of friends who have done it and I always wanted to get better at it. For some reason, that food gave me a boost, did it just have a lot of vitamins or something?" he says with a smirk, he leans his face close to hers.

She fixes her hair and plays with a wisp of her hair, trying to blow it unsuccessfully out of her face. She finally moves it with her hand, then she flattens her skirt with her hands and speaks with purpose as she sits up and moves away from him.

"Well, something…. You really shouldn't bring all kinds of attention to yourself. It never ends well," she says, still struggling with her hair.

"Don't tell me what to do," Xander growls.

He disappears into a puff of smoke, Victoria is coughing and waving her hands in the air, to clear away some of the smoke. She looks around and realizes that he is gone. She looks down at Wilson. He looks up at her and tries to kiss her. She leans down, then pushes his face away. He stumbles, then she puts her finger on her chin, pondering. She sighs loudly and looks in frustration at Wilson.

"Seriously, what an asshole, I'm not going to lie, that gave me a lady boner, but I mean seriously, what a dick." She says, then stamps her feet, then she looks down at her puss-faced pet, and gestures in the direction that Xander flew off. Wilson nods, then flies off in a puff of smoke as well.

The pizza parlor Xander works at materializes into existence. There is a tall, fat, bald, creepy dude on stage, he is holding a microphone, and he is telling bad jokes. There is scattered applause, but most people are on their phones and not engaged. Xander is sitting in a booth, there is a reflection in the window. Wilson is in the alley, hiding behind a dumpster looking in, watching Xander nobody notices him. Xander's friend, John, approaches his booth. He shakes hands with him and sits in the booth, they've known each other for about three years. Xander had been attempting to do stand for that long, he had even hosted a comedy night. The problem with him is that he wasn't that funny, or good at improv. He had no stage presence and was a frightened lump on stage. He could never just be in the moment.

On more than one occasion he said some semi-antisemitic things, without caring that it was offensive. Xander tried his best to fit in with the filth that dwells in every slimy comedy bar.

If he was a pervert and a scumbag, then he would still have his comedy show. His last girlfriend hosted the show with him, took capoeira classes with him, and pretty much did everything he did. When they broke up, they still had to face each other on a near-daily basis. How was he supposed to be funny and in a good mood, if she was giving him laser eyes? Then again, he was never funny.

He was the funniest guy in the room, in his head, but then he got up on the mic and might as well have taken a big dump on the stage every time. That's why he had to quit for a while. How can a comedian not be funny? That's like a tone-deaf singer. You aren't a singer if you can't sing. Maybe he should've just given up a long time ago, but he just couldn't let it go, this was his dream. No matter how improbable it was, it was his fantasy. John yells his name and he finally snaps out of his racing thoughts. John puts his arm around him.

John whispers, "So, can I get some shots for you? I already have a round of tequila coming, how are you feeling tonight? Are you going to get up there?"

"Oh yeah, for some reason, I feel super invigorated tonight, I can't put my finger on it. I met a chick tonight. She made me dinner, and I guess it had some kind of super vitamins in it or something. I feel alive tonight like I never have before," Xander growls again, he is so pumped. His heart is racing fast, he can hear everyone else's heartbeat too. The room blurs, he's never felt this alive. As much as he wishes Sofie was there with him, he can't remember her face, he can barely remember her name. There is one name and one face that he can't get out of his mind. Queen Victoria, she's so beautiful, the way she smells like roses and sandalwood. Gigi, what was the name of his last girlfriend? Genevieve... Gina? Why can't he remember? He realizes that he has been drifting off in thought, for a while. Did John even reply? He didn't even know, John and everyone in the club was on their phone.

No one is engaging with each other, there is a random comic on stage, but no one laughs or engages with him at all.

Xander thinks, "Wow, look at this sad bunch. How has humanity sunken so low?" Xander looks to his right, there is a beautiful, curvy Latina, she is sitting at a table near the center of the room.

Time slows. A spotlight is on her, so that the whole room goes dark and silent, that smell returns, the smell of roses and sandalwood. He looks more closely at her, her eyes flash red. He shakes his head, then time returns to normal, he gets up from the booth,

John is standing next to the stage, he pats Xander's back, then he leans in close and whispers. "So, try not to do any Jewish jokes this time, it came off as kind of anti-Semitic, you know. Be cool. You got this, bro."

Xander walks up to the stage, all the sound fades, except for the sound of a heartbeat, and his eyes lock on to the curvy Latina lady again. He looks into the microphone and breathes heavily. The microphone becomes small, far away. Everything looks like it's inside of a fishbowl. He can hear everyone's heartbeat. The curvy Latina's heartbeat is not as loud, but for some reason, he can't stop thinking about her. Who is she, why hadn't he seen her before? Why is she so enticing? He realizes he's been standing there for a minute. Someone yells, "Say something!" Xander hesitates.

"Hey, I'm Xander," he begins awkwardly. Someone coughs. "Umm, so what's the deal with airplane food? Haha, just kidding!"

People start shuffling in their seats, uncomfortably, and the heartbeats in the room begin to race. He feels a bead of sweat run down his forehead. He is breathing heavily. He loosens his shirt collar.

Someone yells, "Boo, get off the stage!"

Xander continues, "Well, I'm a baker. I bake cakes, did you know that a Chantilly cake that is only half iced is a Chantilly-clad cake?"

There is one guy in the back, who laughs. Someone coughs, and someone else shuffles in their chair. He can feel their awkward stares. Someone boos, but then there is silence. He finally finds the courage to speak. He pounds his foot into the ground, harder than he meant to.

He roars with anger and confidence, "You know, here's the thing, I've got the microphone and you can suck my dick." The audience laughs. "What do you call a trans woman at the gynecologist? Her name is Jennifer, and she has very gentle hands." The audience claps and laughs awkwardly. He calms down and centers himself.

He takes a deep breath and continues, "So, I met this lady tonight, and no I didn't pay her... this time."

The audience laughs slightly louder.

He gains more confidence with every word. "Well, apparently, she turned me into a vampire, or at least that's what she's claiming. I think she was just trying to cover her ass. If I find out later that I have some kind of STD."

The audience laughs.

"Listen, if I find any kind of warts on my dick, and I give it to someone else, I'll just say it's a case of vampirism." The audience laughs. "Just put a small dose of garlic on the sores, as needed, it will clear up in no time." The audience can barely contain themselves." Then, the long-term treatment is some sunlight and a wooden stake to the heart."

He can barely get the punchline out before everyone starts roaring with laughter.

"Next time if I need to protect myself I'll use a condom. Normally, when I jack off, I catch the cum in my foreskin as I orgasm. That's how desperate I am. It's like a perfect little balloon that catches your jizz - a come hither balloon if you will. When I make balloons, I have to watch some kind of nasty porn. My latest craze is women shitting spaghetti out of their asses. Then, I climb out my window, slowly and release my come hither balloon on the bushes. Well, it's safer than trying to fuck some stranger and getting stricken with vampirism, am I right?" Xander practically has to yell over the roars of laughter coming from the audience.

The light fades, along with the audience's laughter. The lights come up slowly. John and Kevin walk up to Xander and pat him on the back.

He is on top of the world. He is drunk with power, the love and admiration he felt from the audience just intensified his power lust. He can't decide if he wants to fuck someone, kill someone, both, or burn down a house. He is so pumped. He's never felt this invigorated in his life. How could this night get any better? Maybe if he had his girlfriend, Katy? What the fuck was her name?

They walk out the door and land in front of the club, John and Kevin are very intoxicated, they can barely stand or walk. They stumble around, then John walks to his car, he fumbles with his keys, then he manages to get his keys into the door. Then he realizes this isn't his car and now he just scratched up someone else's Mustang. John looks around, embarrassed, and runs off into the night.

Kevin walks in the other direction, Xander waits a moment, and then he follows Kevin without him noticing. Kevin is laughing and mumbling to himself. All sound fades, and there is a thunderous heartbeat. It grows louder with each second then Kevin looks behind him. There is no one, nothing, silence. He turns back around, Xander is standing in front of him, his fangs are out, and his eyes are red. He walks slowly towards him. Kevin backs up slowly.

Kevin is shaking as he speaks, "H... Hey man, what's up? How... How are you doing? You did great tonight. Did you want to hang out or something?"

Xander stares very intently at Kevin. His ears become pointy. His eyes are red, his fangs are out. Then it all disappears, he looks normal. Kevin is confused and in disbelief as to what he just witnessed. Is he just drunk, was that even real, or did he imagine it, what the fuck just happened?

Xander speaks calmly, "Nah, man, thanks though."

Xander looks deeply into Kevin's eyes, he feels compelled to do whatever Xander commands, he is subservient, he tries to fight it, but he can't stop staring into his eyes, they are bright red, and they have flames deep inside them.

"I want you to sit on that bench behind you and just chill, why don't you tell me some jokes that you've never used?" Xander is in complete control of him.

Kevin sits, nervously, on the bench, and then he relaxes. He feels normal again. Kevin starts to question everything about his reality. Xander walks around the bench, he massages his shoulders from behind, to relax him. Kevin's voice fades, as the sound of a heartbeat grows louder and louder. Kevin starts telling jokes hesitantly.

"Yeah, umm, ok. What did the toaster say to the slice of bread? I want you inside me. Give it to me! Give it to me! she yelled. I'm so wet, give it to me now! She could scream all she wanted, but I was keeping the umbrella. Oh, how about this one: Two men broke into a drugstore and stole all the Viagra. The police put out an alert to be on the lookout for the two hardened criminals," Kevin says shakily.

Xander is behind Kevin, he bites his neck, blood gushes everywhere, and makes a huge mess. Kevin slumps in his seat on the bench. Xander guides his head down, to the ground. The heartbeat slows. Soft classical music plays and time stops. Xander takes his mouth off of Kevin's neck, then he gasps for air, Victoria walks towards him, she is slow-clapping. She emerges out of the darkness, her scent permeates the air. His knees buckle because of her presence. She is wearing an even more fabulous cloak and dress than before, it is golden, with a long red train. She has an umbrella. She opens it in slow motion, and then it starts to rain.

How did she know it would rain? It can't rain all the time. Xander looks up, everything is different now, the rain hits his face. It feels like little diamonds. He can't feel the cold, it just feels peaceful, blissful. He has no more cares in the world. Victoria speaks and it gets his attention and snaps him out of his haze.

"Aww, how sweet, my baby is all grown up now, he doesn't need to suck on mommy's dried-up, old, leathery teat anymore. Come on, let's go back to the house and prepare the little birdie to fly the nest," Victoria says.

She cackles, then flies away into the night. Wilson follows her. Xander laughs, and then he starts doing Capoeira moves, including flips and kicks. He screams excitedly, turns into smoke, and disappears into oblivion. Finally, he's at peace about... Jennifer, Christina, what was her name? It's not important anymore, the only thing that matters to him is the power he feels and of course Queen Victoria.

CHAPTER 04

Xander walks up to Victoria's room, hoping she's not in there, he pushes the large, old, creaky, door, he tries to be quiet, but ends up knocking over the umbrella stand and banging around. Victoria appears behind him. He jumps and gasps, her eyes are bright pink.

"Subtle. Your killing skills are fairly good for a first-timer, but your stealth could use a little work. You probably don't have a complete grasp on your full powers yet, but I feel like you've done this before," she says with all the sarcasm in the world. Victoria hisses behind him.

Xander disappears, then reappears behind her and strokes her neck, then he breathes heavily on the nape of her neck. He appears in front of her, he goes in for a kiss, and he stops quickly, close to her face. He breathes ever so slightly into her mouth, and she gasps.

"How's that for a grasp on my powers, I'm not sure what you're even talking about, I don't feel any different," he says smoothly.

"So, what you're saying is that your ego has always been bigger than your dick, which I'm sure is tiny. Please, honey, I've met a hundred guys like you and I've eaten many more, you're not special," Victoria says.

Xander turns Victoria around quickly, he grabs her by the shoulders and looks deep into her eyes, his eyes flash red, and then he looks deep into her soul. She has an ancient presence, a depth that he's never felt with another being, for a long time. There is something special about her, of that there is no doubt. What was it? He couldn't put his finger on it, but she just had this aura about her, she radiated a deep wisdom, class, and beauty. Xander tried to gather his thoughts and remember that she killed Angie, Frida, or Colleen, what was her name? He couldn't remember her name, he tried to picture her face, but there was nothing. Victoria was all he could focus on. Time slowed when he stared into her gorgeous, blood-red eyes.

He tried with all of his might to not forget the woman he loved, or so he thought. No one had ever made Xander forget about his girlfriend whom he thought he loved. He was a passionate boyfriend, he adored her, old what's her face. He snapped back into reality, his thoughts traveled for days, weeks, a lifetime, but as he came back to reality, he realized he had only drifted off for a second. Then he was back, looking into those bright, gorgeous pink eyes. Something about her made him forget. He was cautiously optimistic, as this was the tenth girl he had fallen madly in love with, this month.

"How's this for special?" Xander asks with a mission on his mind.

He takes her hand, turns her around, then dips her, then leans in and kisses her passionately. There is a flourish of music and bird chirping in the distance, he stands her back up, fixes her hair, then stands up straight. She gathers her bearings, looks around, and then pounces on him. She rips off his shirt and they fall into her huge bed, feathers go everywhere. There is a loud thumping sound. Wilson slowly creeps in, then his eyes widen, and he starts touching himself. Victoria throws a pillow at his head and knocks him unconscious, without making eye contact.

As they both finish, simultaneously, Victoria falls over from the overwhelming sense of ecstasy. She can't believe how amazing that was. In all of her years on this piss-filled, dirt rock, she has called home for thousands of years, she hadn't experienced feelings like this for another being, in a while. It was becoming more than just a mentor/ mentee relationship. She felt as though he really could be someone to spend eternity with. How could she be so lucky? She found someone to whom she could finally relate.

"That was amazing! I didn't realize how many cobwebs were deep in there, thanks for clearing that out for me. I really needed that! It's been an eon," she exhales between gasps.

They both laugh. Victoria sits up in bed, grabs a bedside mirror, and looks at herself. She is a mess, her hair is halfway up still, and her makeup is smeared. She tries to fix it but doesn't succeed. She gives up, then she feels a hand on her shoulder, Xander is sitting up in bed, he is kissing her shoulder and rubbing his hand down her back, she giggles.

"So, was that special enough for you?" he asks, immensely proud of himself.

"I mean it was alright," Victoria replies, acting coy, then they both giggle.

As he touches her, her whole body fills with goosebumps, she feels her back become warmer every time he strokes her. It is so soft, yet so powerful. She had only experienced this with one other being and he was long dead. Buried in her backyard, with the inscription Laeti Vescimur Nos Subacturis, which means we gladly feast upon those who wish to subdue us.

"Well, I still haven't figured out what you did to make me feel so strong, but tonight has just been so great. I'm going to hit the hay, the sun is coming up, and we don't want to turn into dust," Xander laughs.

"Until the dusk, I shall dream of no one else," Xander says. He kisses her hand and holds it until he reaches the end of the bed, then he gently places her hand on the bed and bows to her. He puts his pants on and turns to the door.

"Bonsoir mon chèr," Victoria whispers, blowing him a kiss.

He turns and looks at her, slightly puzzled.

"What does that mean?" he asks, brashly. Victoria rolls her eyes and looks down at her lap, in disappointment. She waves at him, to shoo him off.

"Never mind you've ruined it, just go, please, I have a migraine. Where is that walking pustule when I need him?" she asks, annoyed.

There is a faint breathing behind her, she turns around and Wilson is there with a glass of blood and two nighttime Advil, on a silver platter.

"Thank you, Wilson, what indeed would I do without you? You are the glue holding my limp, saggy, dusty, old frame together. Without you, the fabric of my guts would be exposed, laid out on the floor, bare and decrepit. All who see it shall feel only pity for a fool, a sad grotto, such as myself. I even have the moldy crevices to prove it."

She sighs with a great effort, then buries herself in the covers.

Wilson tries to kiss her. He misses and she doesn't notice. Victoria stands with much effort and stumbles to her feet. She grabs the wine glass off of the platter and splashes it about.

"What shall I do, Wilson? Alas, he's not the one, he did not give the correct answer. I have this thing that I say to all of the children that I have made. It has been, time and time again, to the infinity, I say the thing, you know, then he or she says the thing and then we do the thing. He didn't say anything, so you know," she cries and faints in the most dramatic way, back into the puddle of blankets on her bed.

After sleeping the morning off, dusk arrives. Xander wanders the streets, it is very misty. If it weren't for the heightened vision that he had, he could see nothing. He still couldn't figure out why he was so strong, had it been the new vitamins he was taking? There was something about Queen Victoria, he couldn't get her out of his mind and now, he felt like something inside him was profoundly different. He looks up and sees a vagrant man drunkenly stumbling and bumping into Xander, who grins. His eyes glow red and his ears grow very pointy.

Xander throws his arm around the man, and they walk off. A piercing scream is heard and then it is silenced. There is a faint echo that lingers in the air. Xander walks back from around the corner, covered in blood and laughing maniacally. He smells the unmistakable scent of his lover. She was very close. Victoria appears behind him, looking mildly impressed.

"Not bad, you can be taught after all. Did you clean up your mess?" she asks while filing her nails, barely looking up at him.

"Not bad? I was fucking fantastic! Did you see all that blood?" he growls, practically begging for her approval.

"Did. You. Clean. Up. Your. Mess?" she growls back.

"Yeah, yeah, I threw the corpse in a dumpster, good enough for the likes of him, right? Don't be such a buzz kill," Xander chuckles, she is angry, he has disrespected her for the last time.

"If you weren't such an asshole you might be doing a little better than these downtrodden, parasite-riddled street folk, but I suppose you have to learn to walk before you can run," her voice boomed and echoed. He blows her off and speaks in a nonchalant voice.

"This was just a bit of fun, lighten up," Xander exclaims.

She can't believe the cockiness in his voice. He has no idea of the ramifications of misbehaving and not abiding by the rules. This ancient energy was more powerful and more sacred than anything he could ever imagine. Then again, Xander enjoyed Kanye, the only good song he ever made was Gay Fish. Oh, wait... never mind.

Victoria couldn't believe the audacity of this ignorant, young fool. How could she have been so blinded by her lust for him? He was no scholar, no intelligent being. He was a phony, a charlatan. Maybe changing him was a mistake, he was starting to evolve, but instead of evolving into an all-powerful being, he was changing into an arrogant douche. This situation was starting to feel very familiar. She's made this mistake before. Victoria takes a deep breath, flattens her skirt, and looks him deeply in the eyes. He feels her gaze could penetrate the very fabric of his soul. He feels it touch something ancient inside him. Something all humans and nonhumans have in common are ancient souls.

"We must uphold our practices, lest we should let pride be our downfall. It only takes one mistake, getting caught ONE time to bring a mob with torches and pitchforks to our castle. Don't get cocky," she says calmly, but firmly.

"Whatever. I'll see you later, I guess, I have to go check on my house," he said smugly.

Xander turns into smoke and disappears, Victoria stamps her feet and starts to walk off, and the homeless man stumbles out from the alleyway. Victoria looks disgusted by the mere sight of the poor fool. She looks at him with pity, until she gets a whiff of him. He smells like a dumpster fire, inside of a sewer. He is drenched in blood and is gushing blood from his neck. He stumbles around and falls to the ground. Victoria grabs his elbow and helps him to his feet. She holds his head as he struggles to breathe, she looks around and sees that no one is around. Her fangs come out, her eyes turn black, then she rears her head back and bites his neck until he goes limp.

"This shithead is turning out to be more of a pain in the ass than I had anticipated, how can he play with his food like that? You have to at least give them a clean death, otherwise, it's just cruel and undignified. From the lowest dregs of society to the highest dregs of society, they deserve a clean death. Even Lawyers and politicians deserve to have it end quickly and cleanly. No, no, no this will not do, I must make sure he isn't leaving a wake in his path. Oh, why must I always be subdued by a good kisser? I have to find him."

Victoria rings her bell then continues, "Wilson, get my camouflage cloak. I have to right this wrong." She says.

CHAPTER 05

Xander is in the club, surrounded by people, dressed like Tony Montana, a lovely young lady is sitting next to him, his arm is around her. He is covered in gold bling. He smiles and he has a gold, fanged grill, he smiles and shows it off. He gets up out of the booth and starts swing dancing with the young lady. They dance, and people shower them with money. Xander is having the time of his life, then he gets up onstage. He is in a dream, everything is so surreal. How can all of this be coming together, what was in that food that Victoria fed him?

He can't stop thinking about her. She is never far from his thoughts. He dreams about her every night. He finds himself having trouble remembering what's-her-face. Did he even care about her? How can he date someone for almost a year, and he can't even remember her face, her voice, her body, her name? How can anyone be so far from reality that he is hallucinating? As he's walking around in the misty night, he hears footsteps, he enters the club and he sees Victoria, then he approaches the booth, and Victoria's face disappears. She is a completely different person. He looks deep into the nameless lady's eyes, there is something familiar about her, yet so foreign.

He had only met her recently, but he found himself thinking about her the same way he thought about... What's-her-fuck... Kitty? He still couldn't remember her name, nor could he picture her face. What a selfish piece of shit he was, he thought to himself. She was killed right in front of him and not only did he not remember her face or voice, but he didn't care.

John is hosting the comedy night, he waves Xander over to the microphone, he introduces him to the crowd. They let out uproarious applause, they give him a standing ovation, and the crowd goes so crazy that the whole building feels like it's going to collapse. Xander gets up to the microphone.

This time when he walks up to the stage, he has never felt so much confidence in his life. He feels like he could fly, he feels the energy from the crowd. He's never felt anything like this before, the room glows with a golden beam of pious light. He stands on the stage for what seems like a lifetime, it was only a second, but it felt like it went on forever. He absorbs the light like a sponge soaking up a spill. It fills him with power and energy, he's levitating with admiration. He is floating on cloud nine from the love and attention he is bathing in, it washes over him like a hot shower.

He begins telling jokes on stage. It's like a dream. He's not even sure what he will say next. The words and jokes flow out with the force of a thousand ocean waves. He reacts to the audience banter with cat-like reflexes. Everything he says leaves the crowd at the edge of their seats and roaring with laughter. He finishes his set with the precision of a samurai who is swinging his sword, in the morning dew. He drops the mic, starts dancing, and does flips. The crowd gives him a standing ovation, the club music is muffled. He is in a bubble and smells the unforgettable scent of his love, Queen Victoria, sandalwood, and roses. He sees her through the reflection of the window, he shakes his head, and she is gone.

The crowd starts dancing and laughing, surrounding Xander in a circle and chanting his name. The sound of the club faded. Xander comes to, after the high of the crowd's energy. He soaks up the vivacity of the crowd and leaves the club. He stumbles out the door, leaning on two women from the club, they are dressed very provocatively. They walk off, then he finds a quiet, dark alleyway, he turns the corner, with the two women. He leans over to one of the women he had been trying to court all night. He acts as if he is going to kiss her, she gasps, and then he leans to her neck and bites her. She kicks in his direction for a minute, then she goes limp. He drops her on the floor. Then, he turns to the other woman. She is screaming and visibly upset. He turns into a puff of smoke, reappears in front of her, and smiles a demonic smile. He rears his head back. His eyes are black, and his ears are pointy, then he bites her. He slowly drops her body to the ground.

He looks up at the full moon. He growls and howls at it like an animal. He turns the corner, and John sees him out of the corner of his eye. John is getting in his car. He looks up. Xander is covered in blood. He dances down the street. John stumbles and shrugs, then he proceeds to struggle with his car keys. Xander turns into smoke and flies into the night. John shakes his head in disbelief, then slaps his face and gets in his car, he drives off. He swerves down the road and fades into the night, like all things do. One of the women Xander had just fed on gets up and wipes her neck off, she transforms into Victoria. She whistles and Wilson appears. She looks very disappointed. She waves at Wilson, and he starts dragging the other woman's body to get rid of it. They both disappear. Victoria is beside herself.

"What a fucking idiot. He's going to get us caught and that will be a nightmare," she says to herself, she flies off and meets Wilson at the castle.

Xander is back in his house dancing to the beat of the music playing from his speaker. He is combing his hair in the mirror. He can't stop admiring himself. He is the most beautiful creature he has ever seen. Queen Victoria who? There is something different about him and he can't put his finger on what it is. Why does he have the drive to kill people? He can't help himself, he needs to hurt people. Before he could barely talk to people, and now they are worshiping the ground he walks on. The very fabric of his being has changed. Everything he knew was somehow different. Now everything is new, everything he knew before is enhanced, more colorful and vibrant than he's ever felt before.

Xander is walking down the steps in his front yard, past a large shrub. He hears the shrub shake. He continues walking and doesn't notice anything else. He stops to look at it skeptically. It continues making noise, but he just shrugs it off and keeps walking. Victoria and Wilson come out from behind the bush. He looks confused and slightly annoyed. Victoria sighs and shakes her head.

They follow him for a minute, then Victoria waves her hand. Wilson disappears. She turns into smoke, and he follows Xander. He stops in the middle of the street and feels his heart is being pulled out of his chest. He follows the sensation. Time slows, the street fades, and finds himself on Queen Victoria's front porch. How did he get there? What was that weird feeling?

Victoria is inside her front room, pacing up and down the floor of her house. She is very agitated. Xander knocks on her door. Wilson answers and gestures for Xander to enter. He enters and finds Victoria in an upset and distressed state. Her hair is not as pristine as it normally is, something about her feels off.

"Where the hell have you been? Did you not hear me calling for you? You know that we have a time crunch, I have certain duties that I have to abide by as a high druid priestess. You know how important this is to me, let's go."

She can't get the words out fast enough. What an idiot! Does he even know the gravity of this situation? She could kill him... again. She hurries him out the door and they both disappear into the night.

They arrive at a lavish mansion. Wilson tries to grab Xander's hand, but he quickly swats it away. Victoria grabs Wilson's hand. She transforms and looks immaculate. She waves at Xander who is wearing a very high-end suit. His hair is slicked back and he can see his reflection in his fancy black shoes. Victoria is wearing red velvet gloves and a luscious, crimson, velvet gown. She has a large hat and an updo. She looks ravishing. She is really beautiful and special. Xander finds himself hypnotized by her. Her aura was beaming a bright purple color with flecks of gold. Wilson is holding three ball masks. He gives them to Victoria and Xander. They all put them on and look as though they just walked out of Eyes Wide Shut. Victoria is more beautiful than Nicole Kidman could ever hope to be and Xander wishes he was as dashing or charming as Tom Cruise. "That will never happen," he thought.

Then they proceed to walk into the mansion. The door opens. There are many vampires, witches, werewolves, and other mythical beings dressed in formal Victorian attire, as well as some people dressed as bats and druids. Many of them seem familiar with Victoria.

She introduces Xander. He bows and flirts with the women he sees. She sees her friend Adam, a drag queen, and kisses his cheek. Xander winks at him, while Victoria's back is turned. Adam smirks. Victoria excuses them. She takes Xander by the arm and talks to him in a quiet corner. She is disgusted, what kind of asshole flirts with other women at a party, in front of his date?

"What the fuck do you think you're doing?" she whispers to him with urgency.

"What do you mean? I'm just having a good time and trying to be polite," he replied, not caring that he was being an asshole.

He made it very clear that he was over Victoria, in front of her closest friends. "How could he, after all she had done for him? For him to be this way in front of everyone, so blatantly... What kind of person treats someone like that, if all they've ever done is be good to him? What kind of person acts like that?" Victoria thought.

"Well, try to be less polite. I am a very high-ranking priestess and you're making me look like a fool for inviting you as my date. Now either you're here with me, or you can leave, you don't get to embarrass me, in front of my people. You got it?" she whispers hastily, pinching his arm slightly.

He swats her hand off of him, she looks shocked and appalled.

"Alright, I'll be chill, I'm just trying to have a good time and you want to make it all serious. All you ever do is yell and glare at me," he says, acting extremely defensive.

"You have no idea what kind of risk I took to turn you. I had to ask permission from the high council. Whomever I choose becomes my royal consort and if they don't approve of you, they will take your powers back. There is only one way to do that, so can you please try to behave?" Victoria stated.

He had no idea or care of the risk and energy it took to change someone into a mythical being. Why would he care? He was riding this wave and it didn't matter how he got there.

"Listen, I didn't ask to be a vampire, you killed whatsername, turned me, and I woke up like this. Besides, I've only been playing along because it's fun to feel something again. I never felt this alive, and I have you to thank for that. You know you're my bottom bitch, right?" he chuckles, not caring about the severity of the situation. He boops her nose and kisses her hand, she blushes, then she clears her throat and straightens herself up.

"First of all, I never said I turned you into a vampire, you assumed that, so calm down, Edward Cullen. Second of all, Yeezy, you know why you didn't fuck anyone else? You have to consummate the ritual with your creator, or else you'll only be half a day walker, even if you make your first kill. We share a collective, all of us, we have to share the power, that's why we have to drain the essence of the livestock, it helps cull the population and feed the collective, the Anu, the ether. That's what courses through your veins and makes you feel powerful," she whispers.

"Oh shit, no wonder the ones I tried to turn melted, I thought I was hallucinating," he says with no regard.

"You were trying to make new ones? That is forbidden, we shouldn't speak about this here, it's too dangerous," she whispers hastily.

The lights and sounds of the party fade, and the room is spinning so fast that he can barely keep track of which way is up and which way is down. The room finally stops spinning. Xander opens his eyes, and he is in a hall of mirrors. Victoria appears in all of the reflections. Her eyes are black. She fades and she is behind him. He turns quickly, he gasps, and then she pushes his chest so hard that he hits the ground. He is falling through time. He sees all of his past lives simultaneously. He can't believe what is happening. It's like a crazy dream, but it's all real.

They are in medieval times. She is a queen and he is at her side near the throne. He looks up and realizes that he is tied up to a chopping block. He struggles and screams. He feels like he can't breathe. Then a masked man raises a massive ax above his head. Xander struggles as hard as he can but to no avail. He sees Victoria sitting on a throne, watching. She grabs Wilson and cries into his chest. The ax comes down in slow motion. It hit his neck, and then the entire scenery changed. He lands with a hard thump on the floor in the hall of mirrors. The room slowly fades into view. Everything is blurry. He leans over and throws up blood all over the floor. Victoria looks at him with disgust, but she understands that when you travel through the time knife it can be disorienting. She gags a bit, then composes herself. She remembers that she is irate at him and begins scolding him.

"What were you thinking, you weren't going to tell me that you were trying to make new beings, do you know how dangerous that is? Some people are too unstable to handle the powers and if you make an unstable being, you are responsible and all others who made you. I should tell them and have them deal with you," she screams in his face.

"Wait, no! I tried to turn them, but they didn't come back. I tried it with my comedy buddy, Kevin. Then his life faded, right there on the bench. The same thing happened with this lady. I had her on my arm, and I thought, what if we could be together forever? But she faded too."

He hesitates.

"I'm the one that screamed in pain, but then I thought, 'Wow, I feel great,' and I left, not caring that everything in my life was dead, just like that. It hurt when they would die, I could feel it."

Xander trails off into his thoughts.

He gasps for air as he struggles to get the words out. He has seen all of his past lives, it's as though in the last five seconds he has matured beyond his many different lifetimes. Xander is changed, now understanding the gravity of what his soul has endured for the last however many years. He saw all of the many lifetimes that he and Victoria were together. He understands the gravity of the situation and that is not a game.

He has been in this cycle for many lifetimes, he always fucks something up and gets his head cut off. Then he has to start all over again as a human baby. It never works out and he is doomed to repeat this cycle for eternity.

"We need to talk when we get home, don't speak about this to anyone. I'm not fucking around. If you tell the wrong person it won't end well, believe me. Just behave and we'll talk about this when we get home. Ok, can you just give me that?" Victoria says with a sense of urgency.

"I promise, thanks for understanding. I truly care about you, mistress. You're different, not just because you're older, but also wiser, deeper, I've never met anyone like you. I'll behave, I promise I remember now, all of the betrayal and lies that we told each other. I'm sorry, I won't do that to you this time, it never ends well, you're right. I remember now," Xander says.

He is still catching his breath after getting the wind knocked out of him when he landed. He stands up and looks at his queen, deep in her amazing pink eyes. He has never really looked at her and now he can see all of the hundreds, if not thousands of years of love that they have shared over many lifetimes. He can't believe that this beautiful woman who stood before him could love him as deeply as she did.

She never had any doubt who he was and that she loved him completely. How could he have been such an idiot? She had given up everything to be with him. The reason she was a vampire, witch, whatever she was, was because of him. She had done it all to be with him, then she turned him and brought him back many times. It would be difficult for this lifetime to not repeat the endless cycle of pain, but she had to try. The feelings they had for each other were genuine and maybe this time, she'd be lucky. That's how it all started, then he would become a cocky asshole, fuck everything up and get his head cut off. It always happened that way. Maybe this time was different?

No matter how many different scenarios happened, different countries didn't matter. It always happened the same way. Her love for him had endured millennia and here he was taking advantage of her and her deep, loving heart. She was more beautiful than anything he had seen in all of his many lifetimes. How could he be so stupid?

Xander looks deep into her soul and kisses Victoria passionately, she struggles a bit but then gives in. Time falls away, birds are singing, piano music plays in the background, and then the party slowly fades back into existence. Xander turns, his eyes flash red and he disappears.

Victoria looks down and gives Wilson a look to follow him, Wilson nods his head and follows in the direction Xander walks off. Victoria walks to the top of the grand staircase in the middle of the ballroom. She nods in the direction of the conductor. He lifts his hands in the direction of the orchestra. They ready their instruments and start playing. Victoria sings an opera song. Everyone claps. Xander looks very pleased. Victoria is kissed several times by many of the patrons around her before she sits in a chair in the ballroom.

Meanwhile, Xander is making his way through the crowd. He hears his name being called. They point to him. Everyone looks at him and cheers. He waves awkwardly, then everyone goes back to what they were doing. Did he just imagine that? What the fuck just happened?

Why did everyone notice him and then just act like it never happened? Was he going mad? The noise of the crowd fades, the light fades, then the only thing he sees is Victoria. Xander's eyes and the eyes in the crowd all turn a bright red, then the light fades. Everything is black, and Xander finds himself in an unknown room. He is holding an unknown woman and kissing her passionately. He closes the door, then he throws the woman on a nearby table. He starts fucking her violently. She moans, and then everything fades. How did he get here? He has no idea what is happening or how it got to this. All he knows is that it feels amazing, and he can't stop himself.

Wilson is standing in the doorway. Xander doesn't see him. His eyes flash red, then a light comes up slowly on Victoria. Her eyes are flashing red, she looks down at the floor and puts her head in her hands. She mingles with everyone for a minute, then she walks down the hallway to another abandoned room. She straightens her dress and her hair. Then she grabs a nearby vase with some flowers in it. She throws it at the ground hard. It shatters. Then there are flashes of Xander fucking the rando lady from the party. Victoria screams. Xander stops for a second, looking around, he hears the scream. After a moment he shrugs his shoulders and continues fucking the woman until he finishes. He gets off of her and starts buttoning his pants. He finds a dusty rag and throws it at her, clumsily. Then he disappears.

Seconds later, Victoria's cloak appears outside of the door in a flash of lightning. The random woman doesn't see Victoria. She is in a cloud of bliss. Victoria doesn't even know her name, and she doesn't care.

What is wrong with him? How could he? After everything that they had been through, after all the love she gave him, for him to take someone, randomly from the crowd and fuck her in front of Victoria? He was so callous and unremorseful. Maybe turning him was a mistake. I guess it's going to be off with his head... again. God dammit. Victoria approaches the random woman slowly, without her noticing. The door swings open and closed. There are flashes of violence. It happens so fast.

Victoria's hand is covered in blood and the lady is on the floor, with her throat cut, bleeding out, begging for her life. Victoria's eyes are bright red. Life fades from the woman's eyes and everything goes black, to nothing, where we are all born and where we all die. From the ether and back we go. All things fade to blackness. Darkness, where we all find solitude. Silence.

CHAPTER 06

Xander is sleeping in his bed, but he can't seem to find peace in his sleep. He tosses and turns restlessly, and even though he is asleep, he can't get comfortable. He has vivid dreams of Queen Victoria. He sees her face, he smells her perfume, and he sees her killing his girlfriend. He runs to her and holds her body. She turns to dust and dissolves. Victoria laughs a most sinister chuckle. It echoes through the graveyard. He still can't see his girlfriend's face. He can't picture it. He is devastated that she's dead, but he can't bring himself to remember her name or her face. How could he love someone he can't remember? The only thing he can remember now is Victoria, there was no one before her or after. Who was he before he began his transformation into a creature of the night, or whatever he was?

It is daytime, there is a small light peeking out from the curtains. There are flashes of Victoria. He tosses and turns in his bed, then he sits up, awake. He is sweating profusely, breathing heavily. Victoria is standing at the end of his bed. He rolls his eyes and throws the covers off the bed. He attempts to get out of bed, but his legs are very heavy. He can't seem to get out of bed or move his legs at all. It feels like bugs are crawling all over him, yet he can't seem to move or do anything about it.

"Did you really think that you could do whatever you wanted without running it by me and I wouldn't know?" she says coyly, "How fucking stupid do you think I am?"

She has a demonic tone to her voice. It booms and shakes his house.

He is terrified, he has never felt fear like he felt when she screamed. He felt it in his soul, there was a shiver going up and down his spine.

"Look, I didn't know that this was exclusive, we never really established anything like that," he says, trying to seem unshaken by her presence.

"Oh, so now this is a misunderstanding? I feel like I was incredibly fucking clear about how the rules worked. What were you thinking? You know what it doesn't matter, you wanted her so much, you can have her, you ate her for dinner, remember?" she says as she cackles loudly.

Victoria pulls her head out of her sleeve and throws it on his bed. He picks it up and freaks out. He sees flashes of him eating dinner at her house. A horrific realization dawns upon him.

Victoria is laughing, she whispers, "You're next," and then continues laughing.

Xander wakes up in his bed, for real this time. He is sweating and panting. He looks around to make sure he is awake. Then he gets out of bed and gets his clothes on. He breathes deeply and reassures himself that it was just a dream. He fills a tea kettle with water and puts it on the stove to warm up, but his hand is so shaky that he drops it on the floor. A flash of Wilson is behind him, then he turns around and no one is there, he's all alone. Or is he?

Later that evening he finds himself at the comedy club. He is surrounded by his friends. They laugh, and the music muffles their conversations. Xander acts as if he's enjoying himself, but there is a heavy fear and sadness in his eyes. He feels like something is missing, but he can't place it. Something in his life is very different, and he's not sure what it is. His head is in a bubble the entire night. He doesn't even perform, he just feels off.

He finds himself exiting the club, walking the same path that he had taken his former victims. It is smoggy and misty in the lamplights. He's not even sure how he got there. It is dark now. He looks at the bench where he killed Kevin. Kevin appears behind him. Xander turns very quickly. Terrified, he is panting. He stumbles and falls to the ground. Kevin approaches him. Xander braces himself and covers his face with his hands. Nothing happens, Kevin just stands there looking confused. Kevin's face is decayed, and his jaw is hanging slightly. There is a hole in his cheek, with maggots crawling in and out of it. He smiles, dropping a few to the ground. Xander is confused and slightly horrified at the beast he has created.

Kevin speaks with a very hoarse and raspy voice, "I wish my grass was emo so that it would cut itself."

Xander looks very confused, Kevin laughs.

Kevin continues, "What has fangs and webbed feet? Count Duckula. Where do polar bears vote? The North Pole. What do you call a bear with no teeth? A gummy bear. A woman walks out of the shower, winks at her boyfriend, and says, 'Honey, I shaved myself down there. Do you know what that means?' The boyfriend says, 'Yeah, it means the drain is clogged again".

Xander stands and waves his hands in the air. He can't believe what he is witnessing. Is he dreaming again? What the fuck is going on? How is Kevin back? He killed him and watched his soul fade, like they all do, how is he standing in front of him? What is he? What has Xander done to his good friend, how can he even face him?

"Ok, alright, that's enough! Please stop! This is more painful than a wooden stake to the heart. I wish that I hadn't heard you tell those jokes. I can't believe I tried to turn you into whatever this is, and your brain became good," Xander manages to say through laughter and skepticism. Kevin raises his hand in the air, Xander covers his face, anticipating a punch to it. He takes his hands down and sees that Kevin is looking at him, still smiling with his hand in the air.

"High five?" Kevin chokes out.

"Sure buddy," Xander says, giggling at the absurdity of the situation. He high-fives him and Kevin's body becomes dust and blows away in the wind.

Xander jumps back in shock. He wipes his hand on his shirt and looks disgusted. He sees the two women that he killed previously approach him, in the same state Kevin did. They giggle and wave at him, one of their heads is hanging by a literal thread, bouncing on her exposed breasts from her torn shirt as she walks.

Xander is not sure what to make of this scene, he steps back from the ladies, slowly reaches his finger out, and touches one of them. She turns to dust and disappears.

He proceeds to "pop" the other one, then he wipes his hand on his shirt. Next, the homeless man walks up to him, stumbling around. Xander tries to "pop" him also, but he just looks up, confused, then grabs Xander's hand. The homeless man's eyes turn red, and he holds Xander's hand tightly and doesn't let go, no matter how hard he shakes it. His eyes grow brighter. There is a loud growling noise, which quickly becomes deafening. Xander begins to scream. Then the cloak on the homeless man's head falls off. The growling ceases and eyes stop glowing. It is Wilson.

There is a loud laugh behind him. It is Victoria. Wilson still won't let go of Xander's hand. Xander finally manages to wrestle his hand away from Wilson. Xander looks angry, but also confused. Victoria is clapping and laughing. Wilson is touching himself in the bush, looking at Xander. He shudders, then kicks Wilson into a tree and walks towards Victoria. She is laughing uncontrollably.

"Ha ha, very funny! Ok, I learned my lesson, did you get your rocks off?" Xander says angrily and sarcastically.

Victoria pulls a small makeup mirror out of her bra. She wipes her eyes and her smeared makeup then collects herself and puts the mirror away. She fixes her tits and wipes lipstick off of her teeth. Xander approaches her cautiously.

"That was the funniest thing I've ever seen in my life! I wish I had my camera out," she says, still laughing uproariously.

"What do you want from me?" Xander yells in frustration.

"The real question is what do you want from me, you don't want to be with me, you don't want my hospitality, my friendship, my respect, guidance, nothing, you want nothing from me. Yet I'm never really far from your thoughts, am I? You can't stop having dreams about me, hearing my voice, seeing me in the corner of your eye? Is any of this ringing a bell?" she asks matter-of-factly.

"Why are you torturing me? What did I do to piss you off so bad? I didn't do anything to you."

Xander tries to understand her motivations. She has to break it down slowly for him, he will never get it.

"See, this is why this will never work, you can't see the bigger picture, you think this is about you. There is no you anymore, there is only the collective, you have to give yourself over to it. The more that you fight being part of it, the harder it will be for you to function in this society."

"Well, what do I have to do? I didn't realize that there were rules," he says, then he crosses his arms and pouts like a child.

"You should've read the fine print before signing the contract. That was your fault."

She laughs again at how ridiculous he looks.

"I was knocked unconscious and forced into this," he yells, irate.

"Honey, no you weren't. I knocked you out before I did the ritual because you kept doing your seizure thing, we are not allowed to turn anyone without their consent," she scoffs.

She takes out her mirror again. There is a glittery, pink powder on it. She blows the powder in his face. He coughs and sneezes violently. Then he flashes back in time. He is asleep on her ritual table. She touches his head softly. She closes her eyes. A light shines from his head.

"Tell me, what is your deepest, inner desire?" Victoria asks, her voice slightly ethereal and echoing.

"To be admired and acknowledged," he coughs out, still asleep while he speaks.

Victoria opens her eyes and pulls away. She looks very confused. She waves her hands and he sits up, suddenly fully awake and conscious. He looks scared and confused. He looks at her and jumps. He puts his fists up like he wants to box her. She swats his hands away and smacks him lightly in the face. She is not intimidated. She snaps her fingers to get him to focus.

"Focus, dum dum! Wake up! What did you say? What did you mean by that?" she asks hastily.

Xander is not fully awake and feels like he's still in a dream. He tries to find his bearings. He shakes his head and gathers his thoughts.

"Wha? Ah, um... I uh, I mean I feel like no one sees me or likes me. I'm all alone, when I do stand-up, I bomb every time because I get nervous, and sometimes I have a hard time coming up with things on the spot. Then I get upset because I can't just say something, then sometimes I say racist shit and I get in trouble," he coughs.

Victoria bursts into laughter, she looks at him with a mixture of pity and amusement.

"Wow, you are adorable! Oh my creator, I'm keeping you, like a fluffy bunny this one. Haha! So, do you want me to help you out?" she chortles.

"What do you mean? I don't have to do anything weird like drink goat jizz or anything like that do I?" Xander cries.

Victoria laughs uncontrollably.

"Are you sure you're not a comedian? Why would I make you drink goat jizz? What purpose would that serve, other than just to fuck with you?"

She can't contain her laughter at how ridiculous he is.

"Well, I don't know, what can you do to help me?" He is slightly nervous at her response, but he does his best to act brave, even though she sees right through it.

"Look, I can give you a gift, the gift of eternal life. Anu will enter your body and it will never leave you. There are a few small terms and conditions, but they're all laid out in this contract. You don't have to do anything you don't want to do. You can walk out right now, and I'll never bother you again. You won't even remember that we met," she says.

She pulls out an aged document. It rolls out, and there is some calligraphy and a line for a signature. He reads it quickly and seems not to be understanding the gravity of the contract. What does all this mean? Is this a business transaction, will he become her slave? He looks at her hesitantly anticipating the worst.

"What will I owe you in return? Is it my soul or something? I've seen the little mermaid and I'm getting some serious Ursula vibes off of you." He snaps. He is still very unsure how this whole situation will play out. Victoria laughs again, everything he says is comedy gold and she can't get enough of it.

"First of all, I take that as a compliment. The drag queen, Divine, who was the inspiration for Ursula, was a demi-goddess. Too bad for her poor unfortunate soul, she didn't follow the rules. Divine was a rebel, what can you do? Listen, if you're worried about it, we can read it together, you get more out of this deal than I do, trust me. Give me your hand," Victoria says.

She takes a deep breath and gestures for him to take a deep breath and calm down. He does, it helps a bit, but he's still very unsure. She places his hand on her chest. All of a sudden, his hand gets sucked into her chest cavity, her heart is exposed. There is a brilliant glow radiating from her, she is a golden goddess.

He feels a warmth that he has never felt, a familiar comfort. The contract is floating with glowing words, he absorbs them into his brain. He touches the contract and a drop of blood splashes on the signature line.

Then the contract disappears and there is a slow breeze that he feels. It gives him a tingle up his spine, and he shivers. Then he feels a hard pulling sensation that starts in his lower back and becomes stronger. Finally, he feels his whole body contorting in ways he never knew possible. Time slows, then speeds up. Xander opens his eyes and he is in the park. How did he get there? Was it another dream? Xander opens his eyes and jumps, he is very startled, panting and sweating.

He finds himself on the bench and spots the blood stain left by Kevin. He jumps up, and Victoria and Wilson are gone. He looks around. The sun has started to rise. A small pin of light rests on his finger. It starts to sizzle. He stumbles, then turns into a puff of smoke and disappears.

Xander wakes up in his bed. He is sweaty and panting. He gets up, lights an incense, takes out his yoga mat, turns on his speaker, and begins a playlist of calming Hindu chants on his phone. He breathes out and starts with the prayer pose. The music fades and intensifies. There is a weird chanting in his head. It echoes. He opens his eyes and hears Victoria laughing. He sees a flash of her in his mirror, then in the other mirror. He rubs his eyes and continues doing his yoga and capoeira routine. Then everything fades. Who is he, is he dreaming again?

Are we always in a dream, what is reality and what is fantasy? He finds himself trying to differentiate, but the lines are fading between what is real and what is in his head. Is he going crazy or is he seeing real figments in the reflection or the mist? What has he gotten himself into? Why can't he get himself out? Is there a way out, or is he doomed to walk the Earth, searching for answers, where there are none? Why can't he remember his life before Queen Victoria? What about... what was her name?

CHAPTER 07

Victoria is in her castle in the garden. Wilson is painting her toenails. She has a moon reflector held up to her neck. She is relaxing with cucumbers on her eyes. She is laughing and enjoying her wine, she says something to Wilson, but it is muffled. Xander is confused about what he is witnessing. "Nothing she says is audible, am I in a dream again? Where am I?" he thinks.

Smoke starts to rise, then the whole scene becomes blurry and out of focus. there is blackness, but it feels like he's falling down a hole. "When will I hit the ground? Will I die when my face collides with the pavement? How far will I fall before I hit the bottom? It feels like I'm falling for years, and then I see the ground approaching fast. I brace myself for impact. Then, nothing. I stop falling. I look down. I am on the ground. How did I get here?" He thinks. "There is a small light in front of me. I follow it. The light gets brighter, and then a door appears. I open it and walk through it. There is a vibrating and a noise so loud, it knocks the wind out of me. I fall to the ground, but there is no ground. There is more light. I begin falling through the night sky. I fall through the clouds. They are stormy, but I don't feel the cold rain on my face. I can't feel the wind. I'm numb to the cold. The moonlight is bright and blinds me, as I see the ground fast approaching. I brace myself for the impact again. This time I hit the ground hard, everything is fuzzy. I look up and see a hand outstretched, offering itself to me. I reach for it. It is rough, like sandpaper and glue. Wait... What the fuck? Eww! It's Wilson's grubby hand. It comes into focus with the force of running into a brick wall at full speed," Xander narrates in his mind.

Xander stands up and realizes that this is not a dream. The garden is still spinning, but he manages to find his bearings. Then he leans over, into the roses, near the pathway and vomits blood, violently. Wilson looks panicked behind him.

"Not the Mistress' roses, they're her favorite. Now she's going to kill me," Wilson wheezes.

Xander stands up and shakes it off, "I guess I'm not dreaming," he chokes out, to himself.

"Mistress wishes for you to join her in her moon bath ritual, it's pretty important, that's why you were called here," Wilson squeaks out, pathetically.

"What do you mean I was called here? I teleported on my own. I imagined somewhere vividly and poof, here I am." Xander says, half growling, his eyes turning red and glowing. Wilson jumps back and cowers behind a rock, near the path.

"Sure, whatever you say, Mistress would like to invite you to midnight tea, would you like some? Please say yes, otherwise the Mistress will kick me." Wilson quivers.

"So, you mean, she's been expecting me?" Xander growls, more aggressively at Wilson.

"Please, my bum is still sore from the last time I made the Mistress angry." Wilson cries.

Xander straightens up and wipes off his mouth, then he fixes his jacket. "Alright, why not? I'm already here," he mumbles to himself.

He continues on the pathway, in the garden, towards Victoria, who is sitting in the gazebo in the middle of the garden. The path winds and twists on and on and forever, then he smells her. There is the unmistakable red cloud of sandalwood and roses, it radiates out of the gazebo, where she is sitting and enjoying tea.

She is wearing a floral-print dress, a big floppy hat, and sunglasses. Nothing could hide her beautiful pink, glowing eyes. Xander could see them through her glasses.

They shine bright in the moonlight, blinding, but also hypnotizing him. He can't seem to look away from her. He is enchanted by her gaze. Wilson reaches for Xander's hand. He snaps out of it, then swats it and teleports to the chair next to Victoria. Victoria smiles, nods, and claps. She is impressed. She offers him her hand. He promptly kisses it.

"Well, now, what has come over you? You're different," Victoria says blushing.

"I just realized that I need you to help me learn to control my powers. I've been thinking a lot about you, and I am sorry I was such an asshole," Xander says.

"Well, I'm glad you finally came to your senses. Would you like to join me for dinner? It's already prepared, we were expecting you," Victoria says.

She gestures to Wilson. He is carrying a tray with two wine goblets on it. He sets the wine goblet down in front of Xander, clumsily, he spills a little. Xander rolls his eyes and puts his napkin on his lap. Victoria waves her hand, the cup floats to her. It positions itself on the table, with grace, very delicately.

Wilson brings a jug filled with wine to Xander, he shakes it and pours some for Xander, but barely manages to not spill it. Every shake of Wilson's hand makes Xander nervous. He can't help but be disgusted by Wilson. He stinks, and his face is as ugly as his putrid death smell.

"How did I get here? It wasn't because of my own powers? It was a strong pulling feeling. Time slowed down, it sped time up, and then I was here," Xander says, carefully choosing his words so that he can get the correct information without scaring Victoria off.

"Here's the thing honey - no one can force you to do anything you want to do, magic or not. If you desired to come here, then you chose to join us. I can call for you all day, but you can always hit ignore, it's kind of like a cellphone," Victoria says.

Xander stands up and offers Victoria his arm. She grabs it, stands up, and walks with him. They walk down the winding pathway, into the back of the castle. Victoria waves her hands. A giant brilliant door appears from pink smoke. They walk towards it and enter the mansion from the back door.

"I'll see you in a few minutes, but please make yourself at home. Feel free to make yourself comfortable. I'll be back soon," Victoria says, then she turns into a puff of pink and glitter, then disappears.

Xander looks around and slowly wanders into a room with a large fireplace. He looks around and admires the decor, he picks up a lamp and looks at it. Wilson appears behind, he jumps, drops the lamp and it breaks on the floor. Xander looks down in horror. He looks at Wilson, he seems unphased, he has a broom and a dustpan, he sighs and begins to clean up the mess.

"Mistress says to head to the dining room, she's ready for you," Wilson squeaks out in a nasal wheeze.

"Oh, cool, thanks," Xander says smugly.

Xander walks to the dining room, he looks back, Wilson is breathing heavily and struggles to sweep up the lamp. Xander laughs as he walks away, he has a confident stride in his walk. He walks into the room, Victoria is sitting at the end of a long dining table, resplendent with red decorations.

Victoria is dressed in a purple ball gown, with a hat and veil. She is eating mystery meat and red sauce and sipping her wine goblet. Xander stands in the doorway, he looks at Victoria and bows.

"Bonsoir, mon petit ami. Ça va?" Victoria says with a coy grin.

"Très bon Madame, merci," Xander replies, and bows to her. Victoria gasps and shakes her head in disbelief.

"Oh shit, I was not expecting that. Wow, hang on one second. I need to recover from that one. Please sit," Victoria fans herself, she drinks a big swig of her wine. She smiles and takes a bite of her food. Xander sits and drinks his goblet, his eyes flash red.

"I will say something, Madam. Your hospitality is something special. You truly know how to make a guest feel welcome, and your food is exquisite," He says between gobbles of his food. It is so delicious, he can't stop himself from gorging and stuffing his face.

"I can't thank you enough for going out of your way to make me feel good. You really are a treasure," Xander struggles to speak and gasps for air as he scarfed down his food as if he had never eaten anything his entire life.

"Why thank you, I've really enjoyed your company. You are welcome here whenever you would like to be. We all make mistakes, and we can all be forgiven through Anu. By the way, have you been learning French?" Victoria grins as she says this.

"No, I have been doing a lot to try to find my center. It led me to recall some of my past lives." Xander says. Everything gets foggy again. The words are flowing out of his mouth like a river. He begins visualizing everything he is describing as if it were happening in front of him. He continues, in a trance.

"My name was Damian, the first time I remember. It was around 1778 and I was living in France, right before the revolution broke out. We met in Paris. I was in a fresh food market. I owned a business, and I was gathering supplies. I remember that I smelled the unmistakable scent of lavender and orchid oil.

That's the oils you used to wear before you grew roses and liked that oil better. I was drawn to a misty alleyway, then the next thing I remember, I woke up in a graveyard and I had been turned. I was a monster. I ran back home, and I discovered an urge that I couldn't control." He says.

"See, the thing about this matter is that it can't be destroyed, so I've been a vampire for a few lifetimes. You always turn me, then it gets fuzzy, and I come back." Xander spills out.

Victoria is clapping and smiling, slightly impressed. "Wow, It only took you a few months this time. Normally it takes you a few years. I'm always drawn to you. I always find you. I turn you, you die, the cycle always repeats itself, no matter what we do. But I can't stop. I've loved you for so long, I'm so glad you remember." She says.

"Of course, I remember. How could I forget? I always remember, right before tragedy strikes. I'm used to it, I've accepted it, that's my fate, I can't fight it, once I discover the truth, I die." He sighs and looks down, slightly disappointed.

"So, I was hoping that we could have one nice night together before I'm horribly burned, stoned to death, stabbed, shot, bludgeoned, whatever you can think of, it's happened to me and I'm ready for it " He sighs loudly, then gives a cheers gesture to Victoria and takes a large gulp of his wine goblet.

"Oh, mon amour, je t'aime. I never wanted to bring you any suffering, I just wanted to give you a good night tonight, I was worried about you, that's why I was checking up on you. I just wish you would've called me, and let me know that you were ok." Victoria says as she kisses his hands.

"I'm ok, you know how it goes, as soon as I remember, things go down the shitter really quickly. I just wanted a little bit more time, until I was ready. Je suis désolé mon petit amour," Xander says, saddened by it, but still there is hope in his eyes. Victoria blushes and smiles at him.

"It's ok, I'm finished eating, would you like to join me in the ballroom, I have a special ritual planned for you. It's something we always do on a blood moon, do you remember?" Victoria says.

Wilson pulls her chair out for her, Victoria stands up and pulls Xander's hands, he gets up, reluctantly, and spins her. Her scent is intoxicating, there is a pink cloud around her, when Xander enters it, he feels like nothing can hurt him. He is in ecstasy. Her aura gives him power and a light he has only ever felt when he's with her. The light fills him, from his toes to the top of his head. He is in her cloud and his head is swimming. He leans in and kisses her deeply.

"How could I forget? Bloodbath, in the moonlight, a long walk in the garden, and then we make love and cuddle until the sunrise. The next evening, I die in a painful, brutal, and completely random way," Xander says drunk on her aura.

"I'm so sorry, I've tried to save you many times, but it's your fate. It's our fate since we betrayed our vows. I'm stuck here too. I chose this though and I would choose you again," She says, shrugging her shoulders.

"Hey, it's ok, really... I've accepted it. I chose you too, remember? It's never going to change, let's just take a stroll in the garden and just enjoy the time we have together. Je t'aime ma chérie," Xander says in a haze.

He drinks her in, all of it is too much, but he wants more. Her power is incredible, he sucks it out of the air and laughs. He can barely stand from the power he is drunk on.

Victoria grabs her umbrella and a fabulous cape, with a hood. Xander takes it out of her hands and helps her fasten it to her dress from behind. She turns around, they look into each other's eyes. Xander leans in for a kiss, and they embrace passionately. Everything is in slow motion. Music permeates the air. A piano plays romantic music in the background, the birds sing out. Nature reacts to their kiss like nothing Xander has ever experienced. Xander raises his hand behind her head. He has a shiny dagger gripped and ready to plunge into the back of her neck.

Before he blinks, he is in bed with her, making passionate love. They are covered in blood. They finish, then they lay there in bliss, cuddling. They sigh and giggle. She lays in his arms. He strokes her arm softly.

"The sun will be up soon. Do you really have to go?" Victoria asks, throwing herself on him and cuddling him.

He smiles and blushes at her and replies, "Only if you don't want me to stay."

Victoria sits up and looks confused at him, "Why wouldn't I want you to stay? I love you! I have for a long time. I chose you over Chodrak, and I would do it again." She says. Her eyes sparkle and glitter in a brilliant lavender shade.

"I don't know. Tomorrow is always painful for both of us. I could go, so that you don't have to see it this time. I love you too, I chose you over Tara and I was punished for it, we both were, but I don't regret it." He says sincerely.

"It helps me know that it's final. Besides, I like to be there for you, so that you don't have to be alone. No one should have to die alone." Victoria says. Her eyes are hypnotizing, he can feel that every word she breathes is the truth. She is so beautiful, he can't break her heart, but he also doesn't want to die. He is tired of coming back and having to start all over again. His soul was heavy and tired. At that moment, he decided he needed to do something to keep himself alive this time, but what?

"Ok, I'll stay, it's going to be messy, it always does." He says, he smiles and nuzzles her nose with his nose. She blushes and they kiss passionately.

"Oh, it's already pretty messy right now, I just came a fountain," Victoria says. She laughs and blushes.

"Oh, I'm aware. In fact, I think I feel some swelling. You're going to have to help me relieve it," he says coyly and giggles.

Victoria and Xander disappear into the bed, laughing and moaning. This is an absolute dream. His head is swimming. He can't stop the things he is feeling. He looks deep into her eyes. They are bright pink. He has never felt love like he has felt with her for so many centuries. It's so familiar, and comfortable, like your favorite blanket. She wraps him in her adoration and makes him feel like he's floating on a cloud. Everything goes dark. Xander wakes up and gets out of bed without waking her.

He puts on his pants and pulls out his dagger. He walks down the hall, as softly and carefully as he can. He sneaks around the hallway and finds Wilson. Xander appears behind him. Xander stabs Wilson to death. There is blood flying everywhere. Xander's face is covered in blood. He licks it off of his sleeve, then he makes his way upstairs. He is silent. He comes to the bed that Victoria is still sleeping in. A floorboard creaks underneath his feet as he gets close to the door. He stops. Victoria stretches, rolls over, and stays asleep.

He moves into the bedroom, lifting his blade high in the air. He tries to stab her, but there is no blood, just feathers. Then she disappears and he sees that he has stabbed a pillow, not her. He looks behind him. There is no one there. His fangs are out, his eyes are red. He looks confused. He hears something behind him. He sees a mirror in the corner. He walks towards it, very slowly and carefully. He stands in front of it. He is shirtless. He looks and admires himself, covered in Wilson's blood. There is a flash of lightning outside and a loud crack of thunder.

Victoria's face appears in the mirror, for a split second. He jumps back, there is a faint sound of her laughter. It grows louder. There is a mist that creeps into the room. It grows more and more dense. Then Xander falls unconscious. Everything goes black.

Xander wakes up in his bed, sweating and panting. He touches his chest, frantically, then looks under the sheets and breathes a sigh of relief.

"That was just a fucked up dream," he says, breathlessly.

He jumps up out of bed, goes to his altar, lights an incense, then rings a bell and puts his hands in prayer. He stands and focuses his breathing. He starts doing yoga. Was it all just a dream? It all seemed so real, but he also had no control. Where is he? Is this a dream? Was he losing time again? How can he be sure? Did he try to kill Victoria? He was so confused, so alone, so cold, if it was all a dream, it was an amazing dream. Why did he have to fuck everything up? Why did he have to wake up? Why can't he just stay asleep? He can't resist her call.

Xander isn't going to die this time. He will find a way to live and be with her. No matter what the cost. This isn't a dream. It's reality and he needed to face it without her. How could he, if he can't let her go?

CHAPTER 08

Some time had passed since Victoria said goodbye to Xander. She reluctantly realized that she had to move on. Knowing him, he'll come back and cause more drama and make her the center of it. It always happened that way. Victoria is sitting in her garden under the moonlight, looking at her phone. There is a dating app open called Monster Mash. She is swiping and acting bored, every few swipes she giggles.

"Oooh, I'll mash his monster balls," she says, then she giggles again.

Wilson brings her a wine glass. She picks it up, takes a big swig, then wipes it on her sleeve. Her fangs are out, and her eyes are red.

"Madam, what are we going to do about the insubordination in our lovely house? He killed me, it hurt," Wilson cries with a slight wheeze.

"Oh, come now, I kill you sometimes for breathing too loudly. Besides, how do we even know he's still alive?" Victoria says, dismissing him.

"Madam, he didn't know I would come back, then he went after you. I would never let anyone hurt you. You can feel it when he dies, and you said you still felt his presence, " Squeaks Wilson.

"Don't be so dramatic, I tasted juniper in my blood wine a few times, after I walked away for a minute. He tried to spike my wine but luckily, I have a sensitive palate, so I didn't drink it. No harm no foul. I also said that I wasn't sure if I felt him or not," she says nonchalantly.

"It just felt different, he was so vicious," Wilson says, concerned.

"Well, tonight we have a new guest, so try and act cool, please. No spying and sneaking around. If I catch you doing that, or masturbating in the corner, I'll kill you too," she warns him.

She cackles. The sound fades away as a monkey-man, in a suit, arrives at the front door. He is holding a bouquet of purple orchids. He rings the bell, straightens his tie, and clears his throat. The door opens, he looks around, then looks down and realizes that Wilson is at his feet. He chuckles a bit, then pats Wilson's head and walks in. Wilson jumps around excitedly.

The monkey man looks around and nods, impressed. Then, a small puff of smoke appears. Victoria makes her entrance down the stairs in a very dramatic manner. She is wearing a long, flowing ball gown. She waves her arms and gestures towards the dining room.

"Good evening, sir. How are you on this lovely moonlit night?" She asks in a confident voice.

"I'm good! Thank you kindly for inviting me. You have a lovely home," the monkey man replies.

She stretches out her hand for him to shake it, but he gently grabs it, kisses it, and bows. She blushes and giggles.

"Well, aren't you sweet? Please join me in the dining room. I have a lovely feast for you," Victoria says, walking into the dining room.

She straightens her skirt and gestures for him to sit at the table. He offers her his hand. She takes it and finishes making her way down the last few steps, he takes her hand and places it under his arm, she blushes and smiles. Then he escorts her to her chair, pulls it out for her, and helps scoot her in. She gives Wilson a very impressed look. Jackson sits at the opposite end of the table. He takes out his napkin and puts it in his lap.

"This is absolutely lovely, thank you so much for your hospitality, this is wonderful." He says in a deep, sexy voice.

Victoria nods, takes a sip of her wine, and begins eating. Politely, Jackson also begins eating. He is such a gentleman.

It fascinated Victoria that someone who is half-beast and half-man is more civilized than a dildo who thinks he's hot shit because he does stand-up comedy and capoeira. The monkey man is so graceful and handsome. She felt something special with Jackson, even more than Xander. She couldn't place it, but there was something about him that felt right. Being with him felt like finishing the last bit of a thousand-piece puzzle

Victoria is totally struck by this man-beast. "I wonder what kind of beast he is in bed?" She thought to herself as they exchanged flirty glances, in between sips of wine and bites of her delicious food. Tonight they were eating pork and not humans. She felt that would be inappropriate, given her guest was closely related to humans, genetically speaking.

Victoria and Jackson take a moonlit stroll in the garden. They are arm in arm. She timidly leans her head on his shoulder, then he blushes. They find a bench in the middle of the garden. They sit together.

"You are really amazing. How are you still single? What's the catch? Are you a lesbian? Are you secretly married? Do you have herpes?" He asks, hoping the answer isn't too good to be true.

"Haha, sometimes I'm a lesbian. The question is, why is a hot, sweet gentleman like yourself still single?" she asks bashfully.

"Well, I'm not sure if you've noticed this, but I am half-monkey, and it freaks people out that I have a tail. It doesn't exactly make it easy to find a beautiful woman like you, who is also interested in a monkey-beast, like me," he chuckles.

"I mean, do people not know that you're a monkey? Do they look at your face?" she asks in disbelief.

"Yeah, but most women prefer me to transform into a full man. It takes a lot of energy to fuck someone silly and hold the illusion at the same time. I've literally been dumped during sex," he says. He turns into a handsome man, Victoria fans herself.

"I have no problem with you being half-monkey. I'd love to be fucked silly. I'm sure that shallow twat didn't deserve you anyways," Victoria retorts and giggles.

He transforms back into his monkey form and raises his eyebrows at her. They laugh together, they stop and look deeply into each other's eyes. Victoria's eyes look huge and sparkly in the moonlight. Jackson kisses her passionately. She laughs and blushes, then they kiss deeply. It's like nothing she's ever felt. Victoria is on a pink cloud of bliss. How can this night get any better? This is a dream for her. She is floating on a pink cloud, then they walk to her bedroom and end up in bed. They throw themselves fully into the passion and make sweet love.

Victoria is asleep, but Jackson is awake. He stares at her, lovingly, he strokes her hair, gently, as she snores, softly, there is a pin of light coming in from the curtains. Jackson gets up, naked, Victoria stretches and goes back to sleep. Jackson looks around and finds a wardrobe with a robe and some slippers in it. He takes them and puts them on. They fit him, he nods and admires himself in the mirror. He sees a flash of Xander in the reflection. He jumps and looks into it again, there is nothing. Maybe he just imagined it.

He walks out on the deck to admire the moon. It is a beautiful night. Wilson appears holding a mug with hot tea in it. He tugs on Jackson's robe. Jackson looks down and smiles. He pats his head like a dog. Wilson giggles. He spots a small patio table and chairs, he sits down, Wilson offers him a newspaper, Jackson accepts it and shakes Wilson's hand. Wilson leaps in delight, then he shakes, happily.

"Thank you, sir. No one has ever wanted to touch my hand. You are much better than her last suitor. He was a real prick, that one," Wilson says in a sniveling, squeaky voice.

"When was the last time she had another suitor?" Jackson inquires.

"Oh, don't worry about him. He was a real tosser. Mistress is through with him, at least if I have anything to say about it. Hopefully, he's dead." Says Wilson, putting up his fists in a very non-intimidating fashion. Wilson scurries off, in a hurry. Jackson opens the paper, shakes his head, and laughs to himself at how ridiculous Wilson is.

Xander is at the nightclub, hanging out in a booth with John, a few other men, and a woman with big, brown, buck teeth. He leans in close and whispers something in her ear. Then she looks down and smiles. They get out of the booth together. They walk to the alley, behind the club. Xander leans in and kisses her. His eyes flash red. He feels a need for blood rising, but he contains himself. They walk to the park together eating ice cream. Xander gestures to her that she has some on her nose. Then she wipes her nose, and he offers to help, but then he takes some ice cream and puts it on her nose, playfully. She laughs, playfully hits him, then begins to chase him around the park.

The light fades, and so does her face. Victoria fades into existence. She is sitting on her patio. Jackson is sitting next to her. He kisses her hand. She smiles and blushes. There are two small red lights near the bushes in her garden. She sees it for a second, then it is gone. She shakes her head and shrugs it off. Wilson brings a letter with a distinctive wax seal to her seal. She opens it and gasps.

Everything fades. Xander is sucked out of his dream and slams back into his body. He wakes up, sweating and panting. Then he stands up and lights an incense. He begins doing his yoga routine. It's the only thing keeping him sane. He keeps hallucinating and having crazy dreams. He still hasn't fully accepted that he is a mythical being of some sort. No one has been in such denial since Cleopatra, who was the queen of "da Nile". Everyone dies, but he's going to fight it with every ounce of his being.

He is outside of his apartment. He checks his mail when a small creature approaches him, and hands him a letter with the same seal as the one that Victoria received. The small being looks kind of like Wilson, he holds out his hand, asking for a tip or something. Xander laughs and punts the small creature across the street. He opens the letter. Music fills the air. Everything is in slow motion and begins to blur and fade. He hits his bed with a loud thud. Xander wakes up in his bed, gets up, lights an incense, and begins his yoga routine yet again. Time slows down. He is standing in the vrksasana, a prayer pose. He concentrates. A bright white light radiates from his third eye chakra.

He chants, "Victoria. Victoria. Victoria."

Victoria is sitting on the patio with Jackson. Her ears start buzzing. She excuses herself and walks into the back room. Jackson doesn't sense anything wrong and is having a conversation with Wilson. She closes the door behind her, she seems stressed and annoyed. She takes a few deep breaths, then they are transported into an unknown graveyard. Victoria looks exasperated.

"What do you want? I was in the middle of something important!" she scolds him.

"Can you meet me tonight? I need to talk to you in person. I have some things I want to ask you about, but I don't feel like being here is going to do the trick," Xander pants and looks around in confusion, he

feels dizzy.

"What could be so important that you need to meet with me right now?" she scoffs at him and laughs. "Why didn't you just call my cell phone or something? Did you really need to use the astral phone? It's like $50 a minute here, only to be used in emergencies," she says angrily.

"Just meet me behind the club, please? Alone, and don't tell anyone where you're going, please, it's important," Xander says desperately.

She can't figure him out. He killed Wilson for no reason. He's not as good of a lover as Jackson, and he is a scum face, lying piece of shit who likes Kanye West and Twilight. How can you trust a douche like that?

"Ok fine, but after this, I'm done with you. You killed Wilson for no reason. You tried to kill me, why should I trust you? I hate having to deal with all of that bullshit. Besides, don't you have some new hoe that you've been hanging out with? I was hoping you would just die already," Victoria sneers.

"What? No. I haven't been with anyone since I was with you. I would never betray you, madam," he says, obviously lying.

Victoria points and laughs at him, a thick, heavy mist starts to appear. Victoria's laughter fades. Time slows, then speeds up again, and Xander is back in his body. He falls over from the impact of his spirit colliding violently with his body. He struggles to regain his composure, the wind has been knocked out of him. He pants very hard. He goes to his fridge, still out of breath. He grabs a bottle with a red liquid in it. He opens it and chugs it. His eyes light up red, then he falls to the ground holding the bottle in his hand. He sits next to his fridge, with the door open. He pants, wipes his mouth and laughs. His fangs are out.

Victoria wakes up and puts on her robe and slippers. Then she rejoins Jackson on the patio. She touches him lightly on the shoulders from behind.

"I really hate to cut this short, but I have to see a man about a horse. So, if you want to stay, you can make yourself at home. I'll be back soon. I just have some very important business to attend to," Victoria says.

"Aww, I'll miss you, mon amour," Jackson says smiling.

He kisses her hand, she leans in and kisses him on the cheek then turns into smoke and disappears. Jackson gets up and walks off, smiling and talking to Wilson. Wilson gives him a tour of the castle and shows him a guest bedroom that Jackson can sleep in. It has a magic wardrobe. He opens it, finding the clothes are exactly his size and style. He takes out some stretchy yoga pants and a comfortable shirt and puts them on. He has a weird feeling, so he decides to follow Victoria's scent.

Xander is sitting on the bench in the graveyard. He is very jittery. He stands up and paces, he sits and moves his legs around, restlessly. He is very agitated. He hears a twig break behind him and turns his head

quickly. No one is there. There is a faint whooshing noise. He follows it with his eyes. He stands and teleports behind Victoria, as she appears.

He is holding a dagger to her neck. He pushes it into her skin. A small bead of blood squeezes out of her neck. Time slows down and she turns around to look him in the eyes. Her eyes are huge and beautiful. He lowers his dagger. Time speeds up and she scratches his face. He wipes his cheek and sees that it's bleeding. He gets in a capoeira stance and begins kicking and flipping around her. Jackson jumps down from a nearby tree and Capoeira kicks Xander across the dirt. He is knocked out cold. Jackson reaches over, gently, to Victoria.

"Are you ok? Are you hurt?" he asks frantically.

"No, I'm ok. Where did you learn that?" she asks slyly.

"I lived in Brazil for like a hundred years. That place is nuts, but damn, the titties are poppin'," he chuckles.

"Why did you follow me?" She asks as she dusts herself off.

"I err... followed your scent. I had a bad feeling. Then, I saw that you were in trouble, so I flew over here," he says matter-of-factly.

"What do you mean you flew?" She asks, confused.

Jackson grabs her and sweeps her off her feet. He flies through clouds, and they come out drenched. He shakes it off, then they land at her house. He sets her down and kisses her cheek. She smiles and blushes.

"You know I can fly too, so it's not that impressive," she says, trying to act nonchalant.

"Well, either way, what were you doing?" Jackson presses her more.

"I was meeting my demonic offspring. He's a real pain in my ass. I'm pretty tired of his shit," she huffs.

"Please don't go see him again. I was really worried. I just love you to pieces and I can't imagine what I would do if something happened to you," Jackson says.

Victoria gasps and blushes.

"I love you too, Jackson. Wilson, get over here right now!" Victoria yells.

Wilson appears. He is very scared and shaking.

"Yes Ma'am?" Wilson asks, quivering.

She gestures for Wilson to come to her. He is shaking and walking to her very slowly. There is a small puddle trailing him. He stands under her and looks up, sheepishly. She smiles at him. Her eyes go black, and her fangs come out. Victoria looks up and sees something. Before Wilson can look up, he's hit with something that sends him flying. He lands in the ballroom and blacks out.

Wilson wakes up on the floor of the ballroom with his head pounding, and his ears ringing, but he hears a commotion in the other room. He follows the noises to the dining room. Jackson is hanging upside down from the chandelier, by his tail. He is holding Victoria and she is riding him and moaning so loud, it sounds like screaming. She notices Wilson and yells at him, then throws something at him. He loses consciousness again, and everything goes black again.

There is a mist and a loud sighing noise, then Wilson begins to wake up. He is in the park. The sun is about to rise in the sky. Victoria is sitting on the bench. Xander approaches her from behind. She moves so fast that she gets behind him in a flash. Her nails are on his neck. A small bead of blood runs down from where they press in. Everything is still blurry and out of focus, but it is clear that his mistress is in trouble. Wilson is terrified.

"How could you betray me? I tried to save you. I loved you and this is what you'd do to me? I could kill you right now," Victoria roars at Xander.

"I just came here to talk and explain myself," Xander says. Both of their eyes are black, and their fangs are out.

"Empty your pockets, NOW!" she screams.

"Okay," Xander says.

He complies. A rubber chicken, a whoopie cushion, a ball gag, and a butt plug fall out of his pockets. Victoria turns him upside down and shakes him, then she sets him down and moves away from him.

"What is your problem? I gave you everything and sacrificed everything for you. Yet all you have done to me is lie, cheat, and treat me like every other whore that you play your little games with. How do you live with yourself?" Victoria cries.

"I was told that if I killed you, I would be able to live this time instead of having to die. I just wanted to understand what it feels like to live, rather than having to worry about how it's going to end again," Xander growls.

"Who told you all of this?" She asks.

"It was one of the old ones. I kept praying and doing yoga. One day he appeared to me and I asked him for the power to stop reincarnating and just live for once. He told me that I already had that power and that if I killed you I would never die. Our bond would be broken for good, instead of me dying horribly," Xander sneers.

"Oh, honey, you got played. What is this old one's name?" she asks snidely.

"He said his name was Rudra," Xander says.

Victoria's jaw hits the floor. Her stomach drops. She composes herself and acts as if there is no significance to his name.

"Well, if you had actually succeeded in killing me, you would still be mortal. He lied to you because he knows what happens when he gives out boons to the wrong being. What do you want from me?" Victoria asks quickly.

"I was hoping you would join me for some tea," Xander says, calmly.

Victoria laughs a deep, demonic cackle. The graveyard disappears and a beautiful garden appears in its place. There is a patio table with a tea set and lovely decorations. He takes her hand, then he begins dancing with her. He pulls her close, almost kisses her, then dips her instead. Jackson is outside the cemetery. His eyes are glowing a turquoise color. He sees all the action through the dimensional portal, and those turquoise eyes redden with rage.

A young woman walks over to the spot where Victoria and Xander are dancing. She seems to have no idea that this alternate dimension is there. She sits next to a grave, looks around, then pulls a lighter and a joint out of her purse. She lights it and hits it. She seems very pleased with herself. Xander dips Victoria and finally kisses her passionately, and deeply. They pull away slowly and look deep into each other's eyes.

"I love you too, I always have, you know that," Xander says in an ethereal voice, it has a slight echo as they speak.

"Why am I still not enough for you then?" she cries. Her voice breaks and her eyes fill with tears.

"You are enough, but right now, you need to get the fuck out of here," He says with a sinister smile and a demonic voice.

"What do you mean?" she says, visibly terrified of him. What is he capable of?

"It's almost dawn, and I figured that if I must die, you should die with me. I never loved you. I lied. You were always so desperate. It's kind of sad," he laughs.

With eyes as black as the night and fangs bore, he pushes her out of the dimensional portal and onto the ground. She comes out of the false dimension, landing on the cold, hard ground in front of the stoner chick with a thud. Then, she gets up and dusts herself off. She looks at the rising sun with panic. Xander appears behind her, grabs her from behind, and forces her to her knees. She screams out in pain. He slams her to the ground so hard that her knees leave a hole in the grave dirt. The sun rises, slowly. She begins to turn to dust as the sun touches her skin. Xander laughs, though his skin burns and begins to blow away too. She wrestles him off and turns to face him. She kicks him in the stomach and blows her hair out of her face. Her face heals, and so does Xander's. He touches his face and looks confused.

"See the thing that Rudra didn't tell you is that sunlight won't kill us. We don't sparkle in the sunlight because this isn't Twilight, you fucking dipshit! I'm not a vampire, and neither are you. You will die when you are fated to die, whether you like it or not," she says, visibly shaken and hurt, but she says this in a tone that conveys that he has no power over her.

Xander is terrified. He thought that if he made his big move, she would be dead. Now, he wasn't sure what to expect. If he couldn't kill her, how could he continue living? He has to think of something fast or she's going to make her move, and that normally involves his head being cut off in a comical, yet horrifyingly painful way. Xander is not looking forward to the repercussions of his actions, but in his narcissistic mind, nothing is his fault. Especially not this. He was just defending himself, after all. The weight of his actions dawns on him when suddenly Jackson appears. He picks Victoria up and flies off with her. Xander stumbles to his feet and flies off in another direction. He teleports to his front lawn, falls, and stumbles up the front steps. He struggles to get his bearings. He falls several more times, then finally makes it to the apartment. His body is still smoking. His clothes are burnt. He frantically pats his clothes until the smoke dissipates. He slams the door, and it echoes through the neighborhood. His body is dissolving and healing itself over and over in the sun. It is excruciating. Xander is going to have to think of something quick or Queen Victoria will strike back. He's sure the only way that will end is with his head leaving his body.

CHAPTER 09

Xander wakes up from a coma-like sleep. His fangs protrude so much he can't close his mouth. His ears, too, are pointier than usual and his eyes are redder. He wakes up hanging from the ceiling. He screams and loses his balance, falling hard on his bed in a heap. He does a flip and gets his bearings, acting like nothing happened. Xander looks around and realizes that he is in his bed. His girlfriend is lying next to him. He is bandaged. His current girlfriend stretches in the same way Victoria used to. He has a flash of the queen, and when he returns to the present, the mystery girl in his bed is covered in blood. He sits up and realizes he is also covered in blood. She disappears, and all the blood vanishes. There is no new girlfriend. What did he just see? Is he hallucinating again? He tries to rub the sleep out of his eyes. A small beam of light comes in from the curtain. It burns his arm. His wounds from the exposure to the sun sting. The fights he had endured left him slightly vulnerable. He hops around in pain and runs to the bathroom.

He washes his face and looks at himself in the mirror. He is pretty beaten up. He sees the vague memory of… what's-her-name? He imagines them in a park, playfully eating ice cream. Did that even happen, or was it a hallucination too? Xander takes a deep look at himself and realizes that he doesn't even know who he is anymore. Is he an immortal god, or just some douche who is stuck in this eternal cycle of karma? Maybe there is a lesson he needs to learn before he can die and be at peace, instead of coming back to this.

He always loved Victoria, he never loved what's-her-fuck. Are those things connected? He'll never know because the only thing he cares about in the world is how he can get what he deserves.

A vague vision appears in his mirror. It is Victoria, cuddling with Jackson in her bed. They are both shirtless, he is playing with her hair. They look into each other's eyes and smile. They look so happy after only a few short months together. How can she just move on so quickly? He feels like he fucked up. Did he ever really love her, or was it just jealousy, purely for the love of competition?

"I hope she doesn't come after me," he thought to himself. "Maybe I should try another preemptive strike, except this time, I'll be ready for whatever they throw at me. I can do this," he says to his reflection.

The vision of Victoria fades. He jumps back in his bed, lays down, and hovers above the bed.

Victoria and Jackson are sitting in the living room, drinking tea. Jackson reads the paper and looks at her, he smiles and just admires her for a minute. She doesn't notice, she's a million miles away. He touches her hand softly and looks her in the eyes.

"Where are you at right now? You're so far away, mon chere," he says lovingly.

"Oh, you know, just wandering, thinking about all the bullshit I've had to put up with," Victoria says with a sigh.

"I was really worried about you, you could have gotten hurt, and I can't be sitting around here worried about you. You need to decide who you want to be with, me or that trash bag filled with dildos you call an ex," he says, a little bit aggravated.

"I choose you. Why the fuck would I choose him? His dick isn't even that great," she says, insulted.

"Look, I saw him dancing with and kissing you and that wasn't part of the plan. You told me to chill no matter what happened, but I can't worry about this again. I love you. Remember the last time you tangled with him? I ended up dead," Jackson says.

"I love you too. I only met with him to try and end it. He's a fuck boy, I want to be with you. He manipulated me." She says.

He stares into her eyes and gives her a passionate kiss. Everything fades into a pink haze. In the distance, she sees a pair of glowing red eyes, she feels him near, but she just ignores him and acts as if nothing is wrong. She smiles at Jackson, then he offers her his arm, she pulls herself out of the chair, she leans her head on his shoulder, lovingly. Jackson smells him too, he looks around suspiciously.

Xander is forced back into his body, as a desperate attempt to not get caught by them. Xander finds that there is a woman in his bed, and he pulls himself off her. His eyes are red, and his fangs are out. He stares at her lifeless body for a minute, admiring what he did. He licks his hand with his long, devil tongue, it is red and forked like his wicked soul. There is a steady stream of blood flowing off of his bed. He grabs her body and makes it disappear with a wave of his hand. A brand new bed appears and all of the bloody mess disappears. He walks to his yoga mat, he begins doing his tireless yoga routine. Many months pass after all of this drama. decides to use whatever time he has left to plan his next move.

Jackson, Victoria, and Wilson are in their ballroom, hosting a fancy masquerade ball. There is a giant Shiva Lingam fountain in the middle of the room, people are going up to it and praying to it. Jackson and Victoria are dancing and smiling as they make their way to the middle of the room. They pray to the Shiva Lingam there. There is a quartet of half-monkeys playing on the stage.

Victoria feels Xander and sees a flash of him in her mind. Jackson pulls on her hand, he whispers in her ear. She giggles. There are many different beings at this ball. A vampire lady, named Fifi clinks a glass with a fork. She gets everyone's attention, and the room goes quiet.

"Bonsoir everyone! We are gathered tonight, on zis lovely full moon, to celebrate our guests of honor, our favorite black widow, Victoria. And Jackson, son of Rudra." Fifi says in a microphone she just created out of thin air.

Fifi gladly presents Victoria and Jackson. Everyone claps, She hands it to Jackson.

"Thank you so much for coming to our humble ballroom. As you know, Queen Victoria and I have been together for a short amount of time, but in that time, I have realized that I have found my soulmate. I called you all here for this party for a reason, I told everyone it was for the spring equinox, but there was another reason. I wanted all of my love's closest friends to be here for this memorable occasion," Jackson's voice booms.

Jackson pauses for a second, he looks at Victoria and takes a deep breath. Then gets on one knee and pulls out a ring box. He opens it. It has a ring that sparkles for days, a huge rock, so big, when she puts it on it will give her back problems. Victoria gasps in shock and cries. The normally composed queen is a mess and in tears. He continues into the microphone.

"Will you marry me?"

Before he can finish, she jumps on him and nods yes. She cries, then he puts the ring on her finger, she can't believe it. He picks her up and kisses her passionately, everyone claps, and some people in the crowd say "Aww".

"What is better than celebrating l'amour nouveau, you ask? Well, I will tell you, when the sacrifice invites himself and tries to hide, like a little pussy cat. Come on up Isaac," Jackson says into the microphone.

Fifi waves her hand and summons Xander to join her, in front of everyone. He was trying to hide in the shadows, but he recognized that this was a trap all along. He was a fish, following their worm. He was summoned to the party and compelled to be there against his will. Victoria felt his presence, she was the fisherwoman, who lured him. As he walked to the stage against his will she looked him in the eyes with disdain. He feels a shiver down his spine. Everyone in the room is hissing and showing their fangs at him.

He couldn't believe this nonsense. He was invited there by a friend, Adam, now they're going to eat him? Adam is on the stage next to Victoria, he is hissing and his eyes are red. He is wearing a long evening gown and his hair is sculpted into a hat.

Xander struggles, but his feet are compelled by an unknown force to walk up to the stage in the ballroom where Jackson, Victoria, and Adam had just stood.

He looks around, panicking, then he is tied up and stripped down. Fifi waves her hands again and he is held by a magical force, in the air, high above the party on full display.

"You see when a baby betrays an old one, we don't take that kindly. We really hoped you would be bon, but because of your indiscretions, you will be punished by ze highest order," Fifi's voice booms without a microphone. He falls on the ground, hard. Then he gets up and attempts to cover himself, still in his underwear.

"How do you plead, mon petit chat?" Fifi asks into the microphone.

She points to Xander, and he turns into a cat, and meows. He turns back into a human. Everyone laughs. She jumps gleefully.

"He pleads meow, you all heard it. Your sentence will be to receive mortality, you will be stripped of all your powers and have no memory of any of this. You will have vague feelings and a sense of déjà vu, but you will be a dismal, lonely pussy cat for ze rest of your sad existence. Then you will keep reincarnating and continuing ze cycle," Fifi tells the audience.

"Isn't that kind of my deal right now anyways," Xander screams.

Everyone is still laughing at him, he struggles to cover himself, and many beings in the crowd point at him and hiss. Fifi waves her hands and quiets the crowd. She slaps Xander so hard that he hits the ground hard. Then she quiets the crowd and finishes her speech.

"Shut up little piggy, you speak when spoken to," Fifi says.

She waves her hands and turns him into a pig. He squeals and runs around wildly, people laugh and try to catch him, she waves her hands again and turns him back into a person, he lands in an awkward position, still in his underwear. He stands up straight.

"I'd like to challenge the verdict! If I win, you will give me true immortality. If I lose, you can cut my head off and I'll come back as a fast food burrito. It says that I have a right to challenge the bylaws," Xander screams in desperation.

A figure appears out of the crowd, he is a glowing being with blue skin. He has a big crown, a cape, and no shirt, he walks through the crowd. People bow to him and make a path for him to walk through. Fifi, Victoria, Adam and Jackson bow to him, as he approaches the front of the ballroom. He gestures for Jackson to stand up. He hugs him and pats him on the back.

"I am King Rudra. I speak for this house, and I wrote the bylaws. What he says is true, but he must have a challenger and there must be a reward to the winner. I nominate my son, Jackson, my pride and joy," Rudra addresses the crowd, not needing a microphone for his thundering voice.

He raises Jackson's hand, and the crowd cheers. Xander looks around nervously and gulps deeply. Xander and Jackson are on the stage. Fifi waves her hands and changes their outfits. The ballroom turns into a fighting arena. Jackson is wearing a button-down shirt, and they are both wearing traditional capoeira pants. The guests are crowded around the ring. Victoria is sitting on the side of the ring. Jackson kisses Victoria and then gets in there with Xander. Xander is looking around, very confused at how quickly this situation got away from him.

"Kick his ass, give him hell," Victoria cheers for Jackson.

Rudra raises his hand to begin the fight. Xander does capoeira moves around Jackson, but he doesn't touch him, Jackson mirrors him in perfect sync. Someone from the crowd tosses Jackson a fedora, he catches it and starts doing Michael Jackson, Smooth Criminal type moves around. The crowd goes crazy. Jackson unbuttons his shirt, he yells, "Oh!" His shirt flaps in the breeze, the sound is so loud. He holds the note. Time slows down. Xander stops flipping sound for a second, then he musters up the strength to do one more kickflip, in the direction of Jackson's head. Time slows down even more. The crowd is cheering. Xander is flying towards Jackson's head. Jackson is holding the note, in Xander's direction the wind resistance is visible, as he approaches Jackson.

Xander falls just short of Jackson. Jackson windmill kicks Xander's face, he flies through the air and lands hard. Xander's face is bleeding, he wipes the blood off of his eye and stands up, unsteady on his feet. He gives Jackson a look as though he wants more. Jackson was working the crowd and didn't even notice. He turns around and sees Xander in the fighting position. He nods and gets ready to kill him, he hasn't had enough yet. Xander windmill kicks at Jackson's head. His head hits the ring, in slow motion. Xander lifts his hands up and cheers for himself. The crowd gasps and boos. Xander is taunting Jackson and working the crowd.

Victoria runs to Jackson's side and picks up his head. His face has no visible damage. She looks confused, then he opens his eyes and winks at her. She gasps and giggles, and Jackson flips off the ground. While Xander's back is turned, Jackson taps him on the shoulder. Xander turns around. Jackson does a Michael Jackson kick to Xander's balls and windmill kicks him in the face. Xander hits the floor, violently. He tries to get up. Xander looks down and gasps for air, he tries to get up, but he fails and falls to the ground, and the crowd goes crazy. Rudra raises Jackson's hand.

"We have a winner, looks like your fate is sealed, you pathetic worm. A trial by combat is exactly what this party needed," Rudra's voice booms.

Victoria runs to Jackson's side. He picks her up, and they kiss passionately. Rudra is blushing and smiling as he stares at them lovingly.

"Now for your punishment, vile creature," Rudra says, looking down at the spot where Xander was just lying on the ground.

He is in amazement, as Xander has disappeared. Everyone's eyes change to blood red. They all hiss and boo. Rudra calms the crowd. They are silent and he speaks with purpose.

"We will get this vile scum and he will pay his sentence. Have no doubts about that. But right now, let's feast and celebrate our undisputed champion and his fiancée! Congratulations! I've never been so proud in my life. Let's eat," his voice booms and shakes the room.

He hugs Jackson, picks him up, and squeezes him. Rudra bows to Victoria and kisses her hand. Then he kisses her on the cheeks, hugs her lightly, and whispers in her ear.

Victoria and Jackson walk to the front of the ballroom, it transforms into a stage with a beautiful, long table that faces the crowd. The middle of the room has transformed from a fighting ring to a beautiful display for their feast. Jackson picks up and carries Victoria to her chair. He sits next to her. It is a beautiful, lavish affair. Jackson and Victoria are surrounded by a pink cloud that has formed around them. Adam, Rudra, and Maya join them at the table on the stage.

Victoria leans over to Jackson and whispers, "Do you think Rudra will get him?"

Jackson scoffs and replies, "Am I half monkey? He's our highest elder and my father. Do you really think he's going to let that douchebag go, after how he insulted you? If anyone is going to find him and bring justice to him, it will be my mom."

"She took out millions of demons by licking the whole planet clean. I think one cocky asshole is going to be an easy feat for her," Adam whispers.

"I love you, let's just enjoy this day and make it about us. We don't need to give that asshole any more power. I only want to be with you," Victoria replies, her eyes a bright shade of pink.

He smiles, they kiss, and everyone claps and awws. A pink heart made of the mist forms around them. They fade into the pink, fuzzy cloud that is their love. The only thing that could mess up this moment is the set of red eyes glowing in the bush outside - the eyes of the human trash bag named Xander, in the shadows, biding his time until the moment was right.

CHAPTER 10

Xander made a beeline for his apartment, he threw the door open, and it flew off of the hinges. He flew down the hall to his bedroom. He frantically looked for a bag, he found one in his closet. He throws it on his bed in a hurry, he rips it open so hard he breaks the zipper. Then he goes into his closet and pulls out a small bundle of cash, a few items of clothing, and a magnum pistol. He sees a pink satin ribbon he stole from Victoria's castle. He loved the way she smelled. He has flashes of the good times with her in his mind.

He fights these thoughts. Then he picks up the ribbon and smells it - the familiar scent of sandalwood and rosewater. How could he forget? He stomps his feet and throws it on the ground, he comes down so hard that the floor cracks under the force of his anger. Then he flies out of the house and disappears into the night with the fury of a thousand chariots. He had never been more determined to do anything than he was to run away from the crowd of vampires who were hot on his trail. He had gotten away and was flying as fast as he could to disappear into the shadows, he was free, at least for now.

Victoria was prancing through the halls of her massive castle, floating on a pink cloud. She arrives at the library, where Jackson is sitting, reading a newspaper next to the fireplace. He's smoking a pipe. His face is deep into his paper. Victoria knocks on the frame of the open door. She smiles. He looks up and folds his paper. He puts it on the side table and looks up at her with all of the love in the world. He summons her to sit on his lap. Victoria jumps and giggles, she sits in his lap and puts her arms around his neck, then she kisses and snuggles him. There is a warmth coming from him that she had only felt once in the thousands of years that she had existed. She had never known love like this, and she didn't know what she did to deserve this wonderful new feeling.

There were only two other beings who had even come close, Isaac, or Xander as he's known in this life, and the one who was her twin spirit. Jackson was her twin spirit. She recognized him the second she saw his picture on the dating app. Victoria was more in the moment than she had ever been, how could this be real? She never wanted this to end, he made her feel like she could take on the world.

When Xander attacked her and tried to kill her, she thought that there was no hope left. Knowing that someone she had loved for over a thousand years tried to kill her, just to save himself, it destroyed her. She never thought that someone she had just met would be so wonderful and perfect for her. She finally found her way back to him. This had to be too good to be true.

She couldn't believe that someone was finally there to catch her when she fell, literally. Every other man had pushed her off the cliff of depression or literally, but not Jackson. He was different. I guess when you date vampires, you expect them to be soul-sucking assholes. It only took her a few thousand years to find him. That's not too bad, considering how long she's been on this Earth.

"Baby, why are you so good to me? You'll never leave me, right?" She asked, tentatively.

"Of course I'll never leave, why would I want to marry you, if I was

just going to leave you?" He inquired.

"I don't know, all I know is that if you hadn't been there to save me when Xander tried to kill me, I could've been really hurt, probably not dead. What if he'd figured out how to destroy me? I've never felt so safe, then when I'm in your arms. You're so warm and amazing, I can't imagine my life without you anymore. There's no point in being alive, or well, half alive if you're not there with me," said Victoria.

"You are the best thing that has ever happened to me. If I ever even think about breaking up with you, I would just off myself. There would be no reason to keep going without you," he said.

"How is it that someone who is so affluent, gorgeous, and perfect, is with me? I mostly date trash vampires and I can't get away from them," she chuckled.

"I love you and I have never felt anything like this with anyone, how is it that you have never been married?" he asked.

"I haven't found anyone that I wanted to commit myself to," she said.

"You see me, for all that I am, and you accept me. I've never known anyone who just loved me for me. You could never do anything that would make me fall out of love with you," he replied.

They embrace and cuddle next to the fire. Wilson walks into the room and knocks the wood in the frame of the door. Victoria sits up and grins.

"Wilson, what would we do without you? What do you need?" Victoria asks.

Wilson approaches them with a tray, it has two goblets of wine and some red berry tea cakes. Victoria gleefully grabs the goblet and starts drinking, then she gets the tea cakes and eats them. They have a bright red filling. Wilson taps Jackon's arm and points at the tea cakes with flowers on the top. The red ones were specially made for Victoria. Wilson clears his throat, he hates giving the Mistress bad news. Sometimes she would kill him out of anger. His little knees quivered with fear and anticipation.

"Madam?" He squeaks at her.

"Yes Wilson, spit it out, what do you want?" she asks, slightly annoyed, her eyes turning red.

"The elders have sent you this letter. They want to have another trial for Xander, and you need to be there to testify," Wilson quivers and holds the tray in front of his face, trembling.

Wilson braces for Victoria to hit him, he shakes and pees himself, like a beaten chihuahua, it is pathetic.

"Goddammit Wilson, I thought you were house-trained!" Victoria yells. She grabs the newspaper Jackson was reading, rolls it up, and hits him on the nose with it.

"Now clean that up, what is your problem?" She shouts at him.

She throws the newspaper at his head. It bounces off and doesn't affect him. He disappears and reappears with a mop. He cleans up the puddle. Victoria is not happy. She throws the letter on the floor and yells in frustration. Wilson was just happy he didn't have to clean up the mess after she ripped him in half again, the stains are very difficult to get out of the carpet.

Jackson picks her up in his arms and flies off the balcony. He takes her to the bedroom and gently places her on the bed. He gets a blanket and drapes it over her, then he lays next to her and kisses her shoulder. She turns to him, and they kiss passionately.

"Don't worry ma cherie, everything will be ok, je promets," Jackson says delicately.

"Yeah, but how do you know? This douchebag has been plaguing my existence for a few thousand years. He'll never stop and even if they say he can't reincarnate, he still could find a way. He's like a fucking cockroach, he just won't die. Trust me, he's died like a billion times."

Victoria says as she hits the pillows in frustration. Jackson smiles and kisses her hand.

"Nothing will come between us this time, I promise, how could he?" Jackson asks.

Victoria just can't believe it, he has always been there in the back of her mind and in the shadows, wherever she was. The thought of something so familiar and wrong at the same time. It's hard to keep a heavy burden like that on your chest and in the back of your mind. In a sick way, it's comforting to know that you have a bag of garbage to dump all of your negative feelings. They share the energy, when he uses it, she feels it and she can connect to, and dump all of her anger or sadness on him. He still hasn't learned to fully control it, it's a constant tug of war. Victoria was normally on the losing end. He loves to use it all up on meditating and trying to kill Victoria. It's pretty pathetic that after so long he still hasn't figured out something to disarm Victoria long enough to take her out. "What a loser," she thought to herself, "I can't believe I fucked him, gross."

Xander hears her thoughts, and he flees his apartment. Xander is wandering in a forest near the town, away from civilization feeding on cats and anything he could find that was warm-blooded in the forest. He couldn't risk being caught near the town and he was living in a cave, like the crazed beast that he had become. The cave was dark and dank, no one could find him there, he was so deep in the woods and hidden under a waterfall. His scent was covered from the other vampires, he made sure of that.

All he could do was sit and bide his time, hopefully he would be forgotten about. Is this truly the way he wanted to live, or would it be worth it to just end it once and for all? Xander was tired of running and coming back, only for him to meet his demise. He would always die most horribly and painfully.

One of the first deaths he could recall was especially brutal. He was placed on a rack, and they split his back open. Then they proceeded to pull his ribs out one by one until he became the blood eagle. Another time Victoria accused him of being a witch. He was inevitably burned alive. The ironic thing is that she was the one doing the magic that she accused him of doing. She loved watching him die every time, he deserved it. He would come back, woo her, and the butterflies would surge inside of them both. Then he would break her heart and she would get him killed in the most gruesome way. It happened every hundred years or so, like clockwork.

Eating cats in a dirty cave was no way to live. Luckily he remembered what to do after they tried to kill you and you have to go on the run. If he wants to be free, it means either dying for real this time or taking Victoria with him. He had never bested her, she's always a step ahead of him. He always met his fate no matter what. How long can he run before they find him this time? The old ones are well, old, if they had so much power, how had they not found him yet? They had all the power in the universe, and yet they hadn't found a simple deplorable freak of nature.

He could smell Victoria, faintly. She haunted his dreams and his thoughts. At times he would wake up, in her bed, lying next to her. He would be awoken by sandalwood and rose water, the unmistakable smell. He missed her, she was never far from his thoughts. He was nothing without her, she was a truly special being. He loved her, he would bend time and space for her. He could feel it when she was thinking about him and using his power. It filled him with joy and pain.

Xander was getting very good at being able to control his powers. He had mastered the art of invisibility, as well as shape-shifting and flying. He had meditated in that cave so much that whenever he saw the sun in the sky, he was never sure if it was rising or setting. He was starting to lose his grip on reality, he was seeing things, hearing voices, and talking to himself. He made friends with a stick that he named Francis. He was the only stick who wouldn't betray him, he could tell him his deepest secrets and fears. Francis wouldn't judge him. Sometimes Xander would yell, "Aids for days" in the cave and respond to the echo.

In his meditation, he saw a blue light. It would speak to him and guide him. He could hear a deep, male voice, speaking to him, giving him advice and trying to help him. "Varada", the voice whispered to him. He had no idea what that meant, maybe something in a different language? He just thought that's what he would call the mysterious voice. He meditated on this thought hard, he tried to visualize what the voice looked like, what it smelled like, was it female, male, neither, both?

He could only get a faint feeling and hear a whisper, but other than that, the energy was extremely subtle. After three long months of being in the cave, he found it very easy to tune into the collective energy. He sat in the cave, listening and biding his time until he could strike. This time he had a foolproof plan, he was going to kill the elders and Victoria. Then, he was going to take her throne and have an army of like-minded beings.

Man-eating, heathens, filthy degenerates, just like him. He thought that he couldn't be the only one who had been rejected by the others. There had to be more like him out there and his next mission was to find them, or they might just find him. The only thing he knew for sure was that he needed to get out of this fucking cave or he was just going to give himself up. He would rather die than stare at these four cave walls, by himself for another second.

He saw his twin spirit at the party. Adam was a woman in a past life but now was a very feminine man. He would wear lovely ball gowns and had long hair and a mustache. He transitioned from female to male with ease. Xander knew that Adam was on the other team with Queen Victoria. They were sisters in a past life and they had always been close. Xander could tune into their conversations about him. They both hated him, the two people who made him the strongest could also make him feel like a little bitch with some hurtful words. He still had some options that he knew of were his siblings. Wolfgang and Estelle. The twins were always there for him, and he knew they would answer his call.

CHAPTER 11

Victoria had never planned a wedding. She had never found anyone she wanted to spend a literal eternity with. Jackson was too good to be true. She kept thinking that the other shoe would drop on her at any moment and she was terrified that this would end the same way it did the last time they were together. Was this the meaning of life? Living for someone else, breathing in their essence, and never tiring of it?

He was like a drug to her. When he would cuddle in bed with her, she felt like she had a warm, comforting cup of soup on a freezing day, in a fuzzy blanket. That moment when you are in a cocoon of hope while reading a good book by the fire - that was the feeling when she touched him or cuddled with him in bed. She could no longer fall asleep or stay asleep if he wasn't there. The thought of him leaving, or not touching her constantly left her feeling withdrawals from him.

His smell permeated all over the bed. He smelled like a monkey, that was for sure, but she didn't care. It was enticing, in a disgusting corn chip and old trash kind of way. When he would leave, she could still smell him, and she missed him. He would only leave for a moment, and it was still too long. When he would roll over, it felt too far away. She woke up next to him and wrapped herself around him like a snake, drinking in his scent and his warmth. He had a cheese and nacho smell. Even though it was not pleasant, she was weirdly aroused by it.

"What is wrong with me?" she thought, disgusted with herself, but also somehow intrigued. He slowly woke up and turned to her. He kissed her and she felt a warm feeling in the pit of her stomach. This is where she was meant to be, in his arms, in a cloud of his stench. She lived in it and loved it. Nothing had ever felt more right in her life.

"Bonjour ma chérie." Jackson said, still sleepy, yawning.

He kissed her again and he felt the warmth in his stomach too, there was something about touching her, and waking up next to her, it just felt right. Like when you work on a puzzle for an hour and you lose the last piece, then you find it on the floor and finish the puzzle. They just felt complete, they could both die tomorrow and not have any regrets, that feeling was rare, and they had found it in each other.

"We have to get up mon amour. We can't just lay in bed all night. We have to do things," Jackson said, rubbing the sleep out of his eyes.

Victoria moans in disapproval, grunts, and throws a tantrum.

"I don't want to. Tell them I died and that I'll be back in a few days. Why do we have to do things, ugh I hate doing things," Victoria protested, flailing her arms around.

She rolls over and gathers the blankets over her head. Jackson struggles to pull the blankets off her. He finally wrestles them away from her, she groans and gets up reluctantly.

"Why do I have to get up? I don't want to be awake, the bed is so warm and comfy. Can't we just sleep for the rest of eternity? I don't want to do it! You can't make me! Ne me quitte pas." She exclaims, sleepily.

"Babe, we have stuff to do," Jackson says tenderly. She moans in protest loudly. Wilson appears with a tray. It has wine on it. Victoria looks down and sighs with relief, then grabs it off the tray and knocks Wilson to the ground. Her hair is in disarray, her makeup is smeared. She sloshes wine all over herself and the floor. She simply looks down, laughs, and wipes her mouth on her arm.

Jackson laughs and helps the poor creature clean up the mess that Victoria has just created. He looks at Wilson with pity and helps him to his feet. Victoria floats down the hall towards the bathroom. She takes off her clothes and gets ready to take a shower. Jackson joins her in the bathroom.

"You know I've never just taken a shower with anyone," Jackson says. "I'm not sure if you've ever showered, period, judging by how you smell all the time," Victoria says.

"I have showered, but typically I just have a jump in the river, and I don't use soap," Jackson says.

"Yeah, I can tell, you smell like an old burrito dumpster," Victoria says.

"Fine, I'll just get your bath ready," he says defeated.

"Oh, don't be silly, this is the twenty-first century. They have these new tools called showers, you should really try it, for all of our sake."

Victoria gestures for him to enter the shower. She pours a few drops of oil in the shower. The room fills with the vapor of the oil she poured. It smells like a wonderful mixture of sandalwood and rose oil, the room is so filled with vapor that it becomes difficult to see Victoria. The mist turns pink, then fills Jackson's nose, he is floating off the floor.

He hears a voice, "Jackson, Jackson."

It starts soft, it sounds somewhat familiar, but he can't place it. Where has he heard that voice before?

"You can't hide from me Jackson, you silly goose," the voice grows louder, taunting him, then, he hears it more clearly.

It isn't Victoria, but it is a female presence. Then the taunting grows louder, it is screaming, and it makes his ears ring. His head feels like it's going to fly off of his body. She is laughing the evilest laugh anyone has ever heard. Her laughter reverberates over and over, louder and louder. Jackson screams in pain. His eyes light up, then his body begins glowing a bright golden glow, he is as bright as one thousand suns. He can't see or hear anything. He is completely blinded by the glowing light and the laughing. He can't focus on anything else, is his head going to explode? The laughter stops, and the light goes away. All that is left is a pink mist.

A woman appears through the mist, she is belly dancing. Only wearing a garland, draped around her neck and a torn skirt. She is gorgeous, she is covered in blood, from head to toe. She hums a melody to him, he recognizes the tune, and then he smells her again. The bloody woman moves closer to Jackson, he is not afraid, she has a calming presence.

Her humming reminds him of when his mother used to hum to help him sleep. There was something familiar about this whole thing, déjà vu. She whispers something in his ear. He can't make it out. It is in an ancient language that he didn't understand.

The mist begins to recede, the bathroom slowly comes back into focus. Victoria steps out of the shower, Jackson is standing in the bathroom, naked, he looks down and realizes that there is a breeze. He shakes his head and rubs his eyes in disbelief. He looks at her, then he looks around and comes out of his fog. Did he hallucinate? What did he just witness?

He feels like he is going on a big drop of a roller coaster. Victoria looks right through Jackson. Does she see him? Does he even exist? Time speeds up, then it slows down, time, then stops altogether. There is an explosion, then there is silence, an eerie silence. Jackson attempts to shield his eyes from the explosion, the dust settles, and then he looks around, Wilson is dead on the ground, his body is in two pieces and his guts are all over the floor, it is a bloodbath. Victoria is gone, he panics and searches for her frantically.

Jackson screams with so much force that he emits an immensely bright golden light from his eyes. He is floating off the ground, he flies up and tries to get a better look at the property. Maybe he didn't see her. She has to be here. He scans the whole castle. There is no hint of Victoria. It's like she just disappeared. He lands and cries. He is devastated. She is gone, and he has nothing to live for. Everything is meaningless and empty without her by his side. What is he going to do?

Nothing matters if she is not here to make it matter. He notices that the pink mist is returning at his feet. He looks up, Victoria materializes in front of him. She is completely unaware of the emotional roller coaster that he has just ridden. He runs to her, she is exiting the shower, and he holds out his hand to help her step out. She puts a towel around her chest. Her hair touches the floor, it is so long and beautiful.

Jackson had never seen Victoria with her hair down. He didn't know how she could be any more beautiful than she already was, but her hair was radiant. It glowed a bright pink color. She takes a towel off the rack and wraps her wet, luscious mane in a fluffy, pink towel. Then she puts her bath slippers on. How did Jackson get so lucky? She is an absolute goddess; how could she want to be with a monkey-like him? The thought of losing her was the emptiest feeling in the world.

Jackson kisses her hand and guides her out of the bathroom. They enter another room. It has a brilliant vanity. The mirror has mermaids around the frame. It is metallic and silver from top to bottom, it has a pink aura to it. Victoria sits at the vanity, she pulls the towel off of her head, and her gorgeous locks glide out and barely skim the floor. Wilson brings his step stool, places it behind her, then climbs it, and begins brushing it with a silver mermaid comb. Wilson styles her hair in a flash. He is putting bobby pins in her hair at the speed of lightning. He finishes. Her hair is in a beautiful updo. She admires herself in the mirror. Wilson moves so fast that all you see is a beam of light. He lotions her face, legs, arms, her whole body. He finishes, then he wheezes and wipes his forehead, which is drenched in sweat.

Victoria nods at him to leave, then she pats his head and hands him a dog treat. Wilson takes it, gleefully and zooms out of the room. Jackson is visibly shaken, his jaw is hanging open, he never expected that little bugger to have it in him. Victoria walks over to Jackson, she breathes on his neck, it makes his whole body quiver.

His towel falls to the ground, and Jackson's eyes widen, he loses focus for a second. Then, he shakes his head and gathers his thoughts.

"Vic, I had a vision when we were getting in the shower, and we should discuss it. I've only had a few visions like that, and they all came true," Jackson says seriously.

"Why, what's wrong, baby? Should I be worried? What did you see?" She is no longer feeling frisky, the seriousness of Jackson's face is concerning.

"We need to call my dad and come up with a game plan. Allons-y, ma chérie," Jackson says, he picks her up and carries her to the bedroom. "I need you to get dressed right now, we need to go to my father, I need his help," Jackson says with urgency.

"Just tell me what's going on, mon coeur. Why are you all worked up, what did you see? Tell me!" she exclaims, her eyes turn blood red.

"Do you trust me?" he asks.

"Well, of course..." she starts to say, but he cuts her off mid-sentence.

"Then you're just going to have to fucking trust me. I'll explain when I understand for sure what I saw. It was all over the place. My mom has forebodings, and she's an expert on these things. That's where I got my power," he says sternly.

Victoria is stunned by how serious he is. She snaps her fingers, she turns to pink mist for a second, then she is in a beautiful purple ball gown. She jumps into his arms, they soar and disappear into the moonlight.

CHAPTER 12

Victoria buries her head in his hairy, beefy chest. It feels like a soft, bearskin rug. The clouds whiz by them as they soar through the chilly atmosphere. Carrying her takes no effort on Jackson's part. It's like carrying a piece of paper to him. She feels so light in his arms, yet she weighs so heavy on his heart. Jackson looks down at her, she is so pure and angelic. How did a cave beast like him get so lucky? He had to stay focused, if anything happened to her, he would kill everyone and then himself, in a brilliant, fiery inferno that would destroy all of reality.

His life without her was a desolate wasteland, a pit of sorrow with no hope left in the whole galaxy. What's the point of existing if she is no longer here for him to exist with? She had become his whole world, the only way to get her away from him would be for someone to pry her from his cold, dead hands. He would fight to the ends of the Earth for her.

They land in a mountain village, hidden deep in a valley. There are many homes built into trees and the mountain itself. The architecture is ancient. It is made from granite and luminous stones that light up as you walk by. Victoria is in awe of this village, it is like nothing she's ever seen.

"I've never been to this village, and I've literally traveled to the most remote islands on the planet." Victoria says matter-of-factly.

"Well, you can't come here unless you know where it is or you've been invited. No one can." Jackson says. He looks at her. She is the only sight that leaves him in awe. The world could come crashing down on his head and he wouldn't notice, as long as she was holding his hand.

The street is bustling with monkey citizens, children, women, men, all sorts of different monkey beings. They notice Jackson and Victoria, the crowd swarm them and make a path for them to walk through. A tall figure is standing on a balcony, high up above the market area. They try to make their way through the market, everyone is trying to get a selfie with the pair and bowing to them. Jackson poses for each monkey person, they are hugging, thanking him and bowing as they walk out of the way. The crowd eventually subsides. Jackson sweeps Victoria off of her feet. He kisses her, deeply, passionately, like it's the last kiss he'll ever share with her. He flies up and lands on the balcony. He sets Victoria down, gently. She adjusts her dress and her hair then she extends her hand. Rudra bows and kisses it.

"What do I owe the pleasure of your company, my queen?" Rudra's voice booms.

"I need to speak to mom, it's important." Jackson says urgently.

"She's downstairs, I think she was watching tv, she said something about tea before you arrived. Would you like some tea, ma douce?" Rudra asks. Rudra offers his arm to Victoria, he leads her in the house, Jackson follows, he races down the stairs. Maya is sitting on the couch, eating a papaya and watching a sitcom. She giggles, then she notices Jackson, she looks surprised, then she stands up. Jackson holds his arms out to hug her, but she slaps him across the face and grabs him by the ear. She pulls his ear close to her mouth, he winces in pain.

"What is wrong with you? How dare you not tell me you were planning on getting engaged." She says very sternly, she lets him go, he rubs his ear.

"You weren't going to bring her here first? What if she's a crazy stalker? How long have you known her, what's her name? How am I supposed to approve of her if I don't even know her name or her family? Is she rich, or is she one of those street monkeys that you used to waste your time on." Maya screams at him, he's a teenager again, being scolded for sneaking out and getting caught burning down the village market.

"Ma, that's not why I'm here. Besides, you could have come to my party, I know for a fact that dad told you to come and that I had a surprise. You were the one that declined." Jackson says, still feeling slightly salty.

"Oh, come on, I'm not going to go to one of your dick measuring contests, normally you and your father are the ones who end up brawling and I have to clean up the blood. No, I refuse to go to those stupid parties, they always get way too out of hand." She says trying to shift the blame.

"Ma, come on, you know I love you. Victoria is upstairs right now. I need your help." Jackson says with a long sigh.

"That must have taken a lot, I know how hard it is for you to ask me for help, I mean you were a chronic bedwetter until you left for college. By the way, why didn't you tell me you were with Queenie? She's been a really good friend of mine for a long time." Maya says, lighting up a cigarette.

"MA! I didn't know she was an old friend of yours, yuck." Jackson yells in anger.

"What, what did I say?" She says between puffs.

"Ma, I need you to do the thing." Jackson says.

"What thing baby? You're too old for me to rub cream on your balls when you get mange." Maya mutters.

"Ma, geez, just tell the whole neighborhood, why don't you yell that a little louder." Jackson says, frustrated.

A voice comes from upstairs, Jackson's face loses all the blood at once. He wanted to run and hide under a rock until he died. His fiancé just heard everything his mother said about him, and he could hear her and his father giggling about it.

"Godammit mom, I'm fucking serious." Jackson says sternly.

"Well spit it out son." Maya says, she waves her hand and taunts him.

Jackson grabs her cigarette and puts it out, she protests, but he grabs her hand and puts it on his forehead. She is transported into his mind, she is walking through his vision, she looks, curiously. She is skeptical at first, then she returns to her body, she shakes off the trance and straightens herself up a bit.

"You could have just said that, you didn't have to make it such a big deal." Maya says.

"Ma, this is a big deal, what does this mean?" Jackson says more aggressively.

"Listen, things are going to happen the way they are supposed to, there's nothing you can do to stop it, so don't fight it. Just do what you know, if you don't know what to do, listen to your instinct, if it doesn't feel right, then don't do it. You're so hardheaded, just feel, stop thinking so much, you'll get migraines again. Queenie is the right choice, trust me, everything will work out. " Maya says, she lightly pats his face, Jackson sighs in frustration.

"Ma, if something happens to Victoria, I will literally destroy reality." Jacksons says, breathing heavily.

"Oh, I know baby, you said that about Francesca too." She says dismissively.

"Ma, Victoria is different, I can't live without her." Jackson says pleading with her.

"Jack, it will be ok, sometimes reality needs a little reboot." She says flippantly.

"Ma, how come you never take anything seriously?" Jackson stomps upstairs into the kitchen, angrily. He grabs a mug out of the cabinet, he makes a cup of tea for Victoria. He reaches into the fridge, puts a splash of milk and a dollop of honey. Then he gently puts in the cup on a saucer, and flies upstairs.

His stomach sinks. His mother is sitting with Victoria and Rudra. They are sitting on the patio, they are on wooden stools, there is a wooden table. Rudra, Maya and Victoria are laughing. Jackson enters the doorway, Victoria turns around, she smiles at him, then he puts the cup of tea on the table in front of her.

"I brought you a cuppa, just how you like it ma Reine." Jackson says through his teeth.

"Wow, you have him waiting on you hand and foot, when he was young, I couldn't even get him to clean his room, now he's a gentleman? I think we'll keep you Queenie, you are absolutely splendid, I've missed our tea sessions." Maya and Victoria laugh.

"I would love my future daughter in law to stay, please, I insist. You had such a long journey. Normally, I think of you more of a sister, but I'm glad Jack found you, you deserve happiness. Well, it's time for me to turn in, I'm a daytime monkey, I have to get up early tomorrow. You are absolutely amazing, and I honestly don't know what a classy queen like you sees in my dirty, heathen, monkey child. I'm glad he chose you; you are absolutely perfect." Maya says, Maya kisses Victoria's hands, she stands up from the table.

"You're too kind Maya, thank you so much for your hospitality. As you know, I have an allergy to the sun." Victoria laughs.

"Bonsoir, Madame, I've missed you and Rudra too. I had no idea Jack was your son, but you've raised a good one." Victoria says. She kisses Maya's hands.

They look deeply into each other's eyes. Maya walks into the house, she grabs Jackson's shirt, and drags him inside. She pushes him into a nearby room, she sits him on the bed.

"Do you have any fucking idea who you're going to marry?" Maya asks.

"What do you mean?" Jackson seems puzzled.

"The darkness she carries is heavy and black. She's so good and she doesn't see it, she sees herself as a monster. You will be the hand that reaches for her in the water, when she's drowning." Maya says, in a trance.

"Ma, stop speaking in metaphors, what the fuck are you talking about?" Jackson cries.

"You know exactly what your vision meant, you're the only one who can save her." Maya shakes her head and comes out of her trance.

"Just tell me... Please ma, how can I fix this?" Jackson says, through his tears.

"You can't do anything baby" Maya says, she sits next to him and holds him as he cries.

"It's going to be ok. I just can't tell you anything else, I don't know exact details, all I know is that it will happen soon, and you will not see it coming, but you have to fight until you have no breath left in you to fight. I believe in you, baby." Maya says. She dries his tears. He straightens up, wipes his tears, kisses his mom, and stands up.

"Goodnight ma, I love you." Jackson says.

"Goodnight baby, I'll see you in the morning" Maya says, she stands and leaves the room.

Jackson composes himself, then he walks to the patio. Rudra and Victoria are looking through a telescope, Jackson smiles. Rudra moves out of the way. Jackson puts his arm around her waist and kisses her neck.

"I'm off to bed too, I'm pretty beat, have a goodnight, buddy." Rudra says he punches Jackson lightly in the arm.

"Night dad." Jackson says. Rudra leaves. Victoria turns around and looks deeply in Jackson's eyes.

"I've never seen Maya act that way. She's really protective of you." Victoria says.

Jackson laughs, "Yeah, I know, my mom still licks my face, when I have something in my fur. She just worries." Jackson says. He picks her up and flies into a nearby tree. They kiss passionately, the noises they make could be heard for miles.

Several hours later, Victoria is sleeping the day off in a tree. There is a small pin of light, leaking in from the shadow of the leaves. Victoria swats at her face, then she wakes up and gets Jackson up. She realizes that they fell asleep during the night and now they were in a tree, while the sun was up.

Jackson grabs his coat from a nearby branch in the tree. He covers her face with it and whisks her into the house, he lands in his childhood room. He gently places her on the bed and covers her with a blanket. He flies faster than he ever has, he makes sure all of the window coverings are down and there is no sunlight in the room. Jackson pulled the blanket off of her head. He kissed her on the forehead.

"Go back to sleep, mon coeur. I'm up and I have a few things that I have to discuss with my parents before our wedding. Je t'aime, bonsoir." He kisses her again. "I'll be right downstairs if you need me, get some sleep." Jackson says, as he rubs her back, she rolls over, sleepily and falls asleep.

Jackson's eyes turn a blood red color, he walks downstairs, his dad is sitting at the table eating a banana and drinking out of a mug. His mom is cleaning the dishes and humming. Rudra looks up, he smiles and stands up.

"There's my little Casanova, you had a great night, we all heard it." Rudra says, chuckling a bit. He punches his arm, playfully.

"Dad, can you not, please, come on, she's a classy lady." Jackson says, annoyed, it was too early for this shit, and he was slightly hung over from being drunk on rose and sandalwood oil.

"Oh, pull that stick out of your ass, son, if you didn't want us to comment on it, you shouldn't have fucked her in a place that the whole village could hear you. I was really proud of how much you made her scream, you sounded like you knew what you were doing" Rudra says, sitting back down.

"Come on dad." Jackson is annoyed with their teasing, no one could ever get under his skin like his parents could. The worst part is they never meant any harm, they just tell it like they see it and they just really care. How can you be mad if all they do is care too much?

"Don't get your tail in a bunch, your dad is just teasing you, but I'm glad you are your father's son, Queenie deserves to orgasm like that every time. That's how your dad makes me scream. We've been together for the last few thousand years. She is a wonderful being and deserves happiness." Maya chimes in.

"Ma, disgusting, now I've lost my appetite, are you happy?" Jackson says horrified.

"I'm going for a flight around the block, I'll probably throw up, thanks for that visual mom, I've really enjoyed this family reunion. Please make sure of no one tries to fuck with Victoria or she'll destroy the universe and kill everyone, ok?" Jackson says, visibly irritated.

"Just be back when the sun goes down, she'll miss you. She's great, you can keep her. Here's a banana smoothie, after you throw up, chug it down, you need your strength." Maya says, she kisses his cheek and hands him a to-go cup.

He sighs and walks off. He flies to a hill, high above the village. He lands and looks down at the village, he sighs and drinks his smoothie. He leans back and stares at the clouds above him. It is a beautiful day. The clouds are fluffy and the sky is clear. He dozes off. He tries to fight it, but then he falls fast asleep. Jackson wakes up. He looks around frantically, the sun is setting, he stands up and flies back to his parents' house as fast as he can.

He picked up flowers as he flew, arrived with a bouquet, and adjusted his hair as he walked in the door. Jackson walked up the stairs, there was an eerie silence hanging in the air. He looks down the hallway and sees the light in his parents' room coming out from under the door. He approaches it and knocks. Maya answers the door.

"Hi baby, you're cutting it kind of close, don't you think?" Maya says.

"No, I'm pretty sure that Vic is still sleeping, she'll be up soon, it's hard to get her out of bed sometimes. I dozed off on the hill, that's why I was gone so long." Jackson says.

"I'm not surprised that you were tired, you were up all night, I know because so was I. I finally found some ear plugs, then I slept, but damn Jack, good for you." Maya says.

"Ma, Geez" Jackson says, he walks towards the room Victoria was sleeping in. He walks in, quietly, then he touches the bed and realizes that it is empty, Victoria is gone. Jackson panics, he screams at the top of his lungs "Ma!!" Maya runs down the hallway with Rudra following close behind.

"What's wrong?" Maya throws the door open.

"Ma, Vic's gone. You were supposed to make sure she didn't leave and that she was taken care of." Jackson says, in an all-out panic.

"Honey, she's older than we are, I'm not going to tell her what to do." Maya says.

"We have to go look for her, mom, do the thing." Jackson says frantically. "

"Oh right," She replies. She touches the floor and sniffs the air. Then she walks downstairs and out of the front door. She stands up and walks to the marketplace. She gets pushed back and finds some resistance in the crowd.

Time slows down for her, Maya's eyes glow, a blinding white color. Time slows down, the crowd disappears, time goes in reverse, then she spots Victoria. She has a hood and a black lace umbrella in her hand. She walks through the market with ease, her face is fully shielded from the sun by the umbrella. Her hands are covered by long, black gloves and she is wearing a lovely black dress. The villagers move aside and bow for her. A man reaches for her hand, she takes it and walks with him. He leads her to a fruit cart, she gives him a gold coin, then he gives her a coconut and she walks to another cart.

There is an alley, she looks at it, something on the ground gets her attention. The sound becomes clearer as Maya tunes into the conversation between the person on the ground and queen Victoria.

"Please ma'am, could you spare that coconut? I'm so hungry, I haven't eaten in three days because I've been banished. I got caught stealing, I was only stealing to feed the young ones. Now we don't eat at all, please ma'am?" the street monkey begs.

Victoria takes pity on him and hands him the coconut. As she does, he grabs her hand, she tries to shake it loose, he grips it tighter. There is a loud screaming, like a very loud bell ringing. Time stops, then Victoria and the dirty monkey disappear into thin air. Maya is sucked out of the memory with such force that she falls to the ground.

The bell ringing is still in her head, it fades into a ringing noise. Everyone's voices are muffled. Rudra holds her in his arms, he asks her if she's ok, his face fades into view, then she loses consciousness.

"What did she see dad?!" Jackson yells frantically.

Rudra shakes his head in disbelief, struggling to find the words. He touches Jackson's forehead with his thumb. Jackson sees what his mother witnessed, then he notices something suspicious. The dirty beggar monkey doesn't look right. Jackson has never seen him, who is he? Jackson runs to Victoria, he sees the beggar grab her hand, then he hears the deafening bell ringing noise. It brings him to his knees. He covers his ears, a fruitless attempt to end the pain of the sound in his head, he looks up and sees a glance of the beggar's eyes.

He remembers him now as Victoria teleports away, there is a split second that Jackson sees the kidnapper for who he really is. He let his guard down for half a second, but that was long enough for his identity to reveal itself to Jackson. It was Xander. He sees a flash of WIlson's body torn apart in the castle, blood all over the floor.

Xander learned how to shapeshift and teleport, and he took Victoria. Jackson comes out of the vision, he is screaming, holding his mother, her body is completely limp.

"Dad, get mom inside, we're going to war. This motherfucker asked for it, he's going to get it." Jackson says. He flies to the top of a high statue in the town square, his voice booms.

"I'm calling to you, citizens of Svarga. I am calling to you in our time of need. I ask you to take up arms, anyone who wants to fight to bring our future queen home. She has been kidnapped by an imposter, he is torturing her and trying to figure out how to kill her. We must get her back, she is my world, my universe, please help me, I beg you." He screams for the whole village to hear.

He feels discouraged, no one responds at first. Then there is a low chanting noise. The noise grows louder and louder as Jackson flies down to the middle of the town square. The villagers surround him, chanting and making noise, they lift him up and cheer for him.

There is a war coming, like no war the world has ever seen, now he must face his destiny, he will fight to the ends of the Earth for Victoria and now it's time to put his money where his mouth is. The time to act is now.

CHAPTER 13

Jackson arrives back at the castle with his father and an army of monkey people following him. They are riding on bright, golden griffins, some are red, blue, and all kinds of colors. They all land in the courtyard, in the rose garden. They find Jackson, on his knees, crying, he is in the middle of the garden. Bandit is sitting next to him, trying to get his attention, Jackson pets him and then shows him off. He is standing in the gazebo. It has many dazzling stained glass windows. He is kneeling near a bench, he has flashes of him and Victoria sitting there, kissing, and drinking tea.

Rudra walks into the entrance and sees that there is a large crevice in the tiles underneath Jackson. He had smashed the floor so hard that you could see the dirt under the tiles that were placed in the garden. They used to resemble a checkerboard, but now they were completely destroyed.

There were bits of floor in some nearby bushes, strewn everywhere, Rudra whispers something to his right-hand man. He was a tall, muscular, blue, flying boar, named Moccus. Jackson's vision was beginning to blur, everything around him was spinning. As he looked into Moccus's eyes, he had flashes of his childhood. His father was eating dinner, then Moccus would come in and say it was urgent, then dad would leave, and he wouldn't come back for many days if not weeks, but he always came back.

Moccus was always there by his side when he returned, his most trusted advisor. Yet, there was nothing he could do to bring Victoria back. He always knew the solution. How can you find an answer to a question when you don't know what to ask?

Jackson's vision comes back into focus, he hears Moccus tell everyone to get back, but it is muffled and there is an ear-shattering ringing, that's all he can hear.

The sound is so loud that he can see the soundwaves reverberating through the air, his vision becomes distorted with every wave that pulsates through his whole body. He clutches his chest, the weight of the vibrations is so heavy. He can't find the strength to lift himself off the ground. He sees flashes of him and Victoria taking a late-night stroll and drinking tea. She leans her head into his shoulder, then he kisses her hand.

He comes back to reality instantaneously; he screams with the force of a nuclear bomb going off. His eyes radiate a blazing white beam, it lights up the whole garden, and his screams let off a shockwave of wind. The force shatters the windows, and the glass-stained art flies everywhere. The monkey people outside of the gazebo hide behind bushes for cover, some retain small cuts on their faces and hands. Jackson loses consciousness and falls to the ground.

Rudra runs to his son's aid. He picks him up and flies through the roof of the gazebo. He leaves a huge mess in his wake. Then he lands at the front door, which is open slightly. Rudra pushes it open and enters, still holding Jackson in his arms. He knocks on the open door.

"Is anyone here? Where is that freaky little weirdo, what was his name? Richard, Michael?"

Rudra snaps his fingers, "William, I think that's it!"

He yells down the hallway, it echoes and reverberates, making the walls shake and sending a wind current, from the force of his voice.

"William, are you here?" Rudra yells.

He flies down the hallway, holding his unconscious son. He finds a bedroom, he enters it. Jackson's vision is cloudy, he feels himself falling in and out of consciousness. As he fades in, he notices that they are in

Victoria's bedroom, he has flashes of them fucking and sleeping. All the lovely memories that they shared in this room; he can still smell her. Then he fades into reality and sees Wilson lying on the floor, dead, exactly like his vision. It had come true.

He leaps out of Rudra's arms. There is blood soaking the wooden floors. The wallpaper is stained with his blood and brain matter, it is all over the room, but somehow didn't touch the bed. The bed that Jackson had many great and loving memories with Vic, the way she smelled, the way her soft skin caressed his coarse fur. Now it was empty, that's how it felt without her there with him, empty and all alone.

"Son, are you ok? You passed out after you destroyed the gazebo outside." Rudra says his voice is barely audible.

Jackson begins to lose consciousness again. Rudra runs and catches him; he lays him in the bed that he and Victoria share and tucks him in. Rudra sees flashes of him tucking Jackson into his bed as a child. He will always see his son as his baby, no matter how old or mature he gets. Jackson falls into a deep sleep and is snoring very loudly. Rudra smiles and picks up Wilson's body, then he leaves the room.

Rudra holds Wilson's legs in one hand and his torso in the other. He stuffs his organs back into his torso the best that he can, then he takes the two halves and smashes them together, they light up with a blue hue, and they fuse. Wilson looks up at Rudra, confused.

"What are you doing here, your highness? How long have I been dead?" Wilson inquires.

"I'm not sure, but I need you to come with me and help me with something," Rudra explains.

"Anything you need, your greatness," Wilson says bowing to him.

"Oh no need for that, call me Rudra," Rudra says chuckling.

"Anything you need, Master Rudra, I'm your loyal servant," Wilson whimpers.

"Good, come with me," Rudra says.

He pats Wilson's back so hard that he knocks him over, he laughs and then rushes to help him up.

"Sorry about that, buddy, let me help you out," Rudra says between giggles.

Rudra picks Wilson up and places him on his shoulder. Wilson sits and is in awe. He has never been picked up. He has always waited on the mistress and anyone she invited over. Now he was being carried by a god who could fly. Wilson had never flown.

The wind was in his hair. He had never felt so free. He makes a pathetic squeak saying, "WHEEEE!"

Rudra laughs, he is very amused by this odd tiny creature. They arrive in the garden where the rest of the tribe is still hiding out of fear of any more explosions.

Moccus is tending to the villagers' cuts and abrasions. He places his hands on their wounds and heals them with a luminous green light. Rudra approaches him, he finishes healing one of the villagers, and then he waves at the monkey to go away.

"What did you find in the castle?" Moccus asks, shaking his hands off.

"Well, this little guy was torn in half in Queenie's bedroom. I think that fucking poser, sparkly vampire, Xander Cullen murdered our little buddy here. Jack is asleep, I put him to bed, he needs to rest, he's been through a lot today," Rudra says.

"So, what's the plan? We must go after him. He took Queenie. She was going to become part of the family. We have to save her, he declared war on us. Anyone of us could be next," Moccus says with urgency.

"You think I don't know that? Xander has always done this, then she falls for him and he fucks everyone over. I had no idea that Jack was her match, but I'm glad that it's someone we know is good for her," Rudra retorts, slightly aggressively.

"I'm just saying that I think we should take the night to plan our counterstrike on this asshole. Who knows how he got the powers that he obtained? Who knows what kind of power he has? We can't go in there blind; he could kill everyone, and we need Jack," Moccus says, trying to cool the situation.

Rudra sets Wilson on the ground, pats his tiny head, and looks at him like a little, ugly, old, deformed dog.

"Master Rudra, I can tell you what happened," Wilson squeaks.

Rudra smiles.

"We'll get to that in a minute, I need you to do something for me. We're going to stay in the castle for a little while. I need you to accommodate my people, get them food, a room, whatever they need. And please keep an eye on my son, Jack," Rudra says as he towers over Wilson.

"Anything you need my lord, but the thing is, Xander told me everything before he killed me," Wilson wheezes.

"Well, what did he say, little one? Come on, speak up now," Moccus says.

"He came in after Master Jackson and Mistress left. I was tidying up, after dinner, they said that they would only be gone a few days and I wanted to make sure the castle was in good condition for when she came back. I saw that the front door was ajar," He wheezes.

"I thought the mistress forgot to close it. So, I shut it and went to the Mistress' room. He was standing near the mirror, it looked like he was doing yoga or something. Then he grabbed me and held me off the ground by my neck. He was moving very fast. He asked me where she was and I told him that they left right before he got there. Then, he said that he was going to take down the whole society that mocked him. He also said that he had his army of rejects. He told me that he had been given these powers by a mysterious spirit. Then he ripped me in half. The next thing I know is Master Rudra holding me," Wilson says, slightly breathless.

"He must have followed them, but how did he get into the village? Outsiders are not able to penetrate the force field," Moccus says.

"I'm not sure, but we're going to have to do some more research on what kind of powers he has and how many soldiers he has on his side," Rudra says.

He turns to Wilson, "Did he say who gave him his powers? A name, description, anything?" Rudra asks.

"No, he just said Varada guides him and that he channels his powers through the ether," Wilson says.

"Are you fucking kidding me? Varada, really? So, this is a more desperate situation than we realized!" Moccus yells.

"Great, so this just went from a kidnapping to a potential ending of the world situation, this is not what I needed to fucking hear. My son is going to freak out, we need to keep him calm. Come with me, mon peur, we need to prepare," Rudra says seriously.

Rudra picks Wilson up and flies off. Moccus returns to the troops in the garden. They are all still confused and waiting for command. The monkeys are cleaning up the destruction that Jackson left in his wake.

"Everyone, please make your way to the castle and look for a vacant room, please do not disturb Prince Jackson. He needs to rest. If you find his room, please leave him alone and let him sleep. King's orders, go get comfortable and rest up. I need some volunteers to help me set up our camp out here in the yard. Thanks, everyone!" Moccus yells loudly enough for everyone in the garden to hear.

Three monkey people approach Moccus. There was a great diversity of species and colors of monkey-folk.

Jackson is sleeping and snoring loudly in the bedroom. He tosses and turns. He is not having a peaceful sleep like he did when she was there with him. He sees Victoria chained in a cave, filthy, her dress is torn, her makeup is smeared, and her hair is a wild mess on her head. She is crying and is sitting with her head on her knees. She looks up from her corner, her eyes a bright red. Then Xander appears in the shadows. He smiles a devilish grin. His fangs are out, and his eyes are red too.

"What do you want from me? I'll give you whatever you want, name it, just please, don't hurt Jack!" Victoria says through sobs. "I love him so much, please, he didn't do anything, don't hurt him, do whatever you want to me. I just want to be with Jack, please, Xander. Let me go!" She sobs.

He stands silently for a moment, then Xander growls, "I don't want anything from you. I want to kill all your little friends in your stupid fucking society. I won't stand for humiliation like that. They will all pay for laughing at me and you will pay for turning me into whatever I am."

"You're not a man, you act like a child who is throwing a tantrum and making it everyone else's problem," she says.

"See that's where you're wrong, your highness! It IS your problem. I think I've figured out how I'm going to kill you, but I need your man to be involved or else it won't work. I found your one weakness." Xander threatens.

"Oh yeah, and what is that, Xander Cullen? The sun isn't it, what else did you find out?" She asks, daring him.

Xander pulls a hot poker out of a fire that is burning near her. He points it at her face. "This is not an ordinary fire. It is Agni fire, from the flames of eternity. I have been doing some research and it turns out there is a way to kill an immortal goddess," Xander whispers.

He stabs her in the stomach with the poker, and she screams a horrible scream.

"It's not this. This just hurts you, I just want to watch you squirm while we wait for your real weakness," Xander says he stabs her a few more times.

Jackson wakes up and jumps out of bed. A few soldiers wander through the hall, but Jackson pushes them out of the way. He finds his father in the ballroom.

"Dad, I really need to talk to you," Jackson says.

Rudra is talking to a marmoset. He whispers something to him, then exits the ballroom. Rudra pats Jackson on the back.

"You should be resting son. You've had a really hard day," Rudra says to Jackson.

"Dad, I had another vision, Xander is torturing her with Agni fire, and he said he knows how to kill her, it's only a matter of time," Jackson says.

"I already know. We have intel on how we're going to get him and save Queenie. This isn't my first war. We'll save her, I promise," Rudra says.

"Dad, please, he's hurting her!" Jackson cries.

Maya enters the ballroom and rushes over to Jackson, she hugs him and holds him tight.

"Ma, what are you doing here? I thought you never involved yourself in these affairs?" Jackson asks, stunned.

"This is different, your dad needed me to help retrace dipshit's steps, we'll get her back baby, I know we will, she'll be ok. She's survived this long without you, and she's tough," Maya says, rubbing his cheek.

"Ma, he's hurting her, I saw it," Jackson says.

"I know baby, I saw it too, but your dad has a plan. It will all work out. Come with me, we need to get some food together for our tribe. They're getting hungry and restless" Maya says.

She wipes the tears from his face and leads him out of the ballroom. Moccus enters after she leaves, and approaches Rudra.

"He's too close to this," Moccus says to Rudra.

"I know. But his heart is in the right place, and we are going to get her back, of that I'm certain," Rudra says.

"We're going to war and I'm not sure we're ready for it," Moccus says.

Rudra sighs, "When have we ever been? This is no different than any other battle. We will win, or everyone will die. We don't have a choice. We have to fight, or we'll die."

CHAPTER 14

After Xander escaped the party, he spent his time watching everything that Victoria and Jackson had been up to for the last year, by tuning into her energy and receiving visions of her memories. He was always in the shadows, lurking, waiting for his moment to pounce. The moment when she was vulnerable and her guard was down, he took her. His plan worked flawlessly. He sat in the corner of their garden while they danced in the moonlight, in his vision. They looked so happy it made Xander physically ill.

"How can she just drop the feelings that she had for me and just move on like that?" he thought. He watched her memories every night. Fortunately, he knew how to channel her thoughts without having to be there. He could see everything. Every pet name, kiss, and minute that they spent on a cloud of bliss he was there, always watching them.

He would come out of his visions and eat a delicious cave rat, he was still dwelling in the cave. It gave him power, taking the life of another and harnessing its energy to sustain himself. The blood ran down his mouth, spilling down his neck and his chest. After getting his fill of cave pests, he would turn his attention to the energy he had been following. It whispered things to him, gave him commands, and taught him how to use his powers.

He would begin his yoga routine. He would see the smoke from the incense slow down, as time itself slowed. Then he would pick up his scimitar and cut off his own head. The blood painted the walls of the cave. He did this routine all night, every night. He never slept nor rested. He simply cut off his head and his body would lay there, limp for many minutes until he would claw his way back from death.

He would sew his head back on and then it would mend itself. As soon as it would, he would repeat this process.

On and on, he lost track of how long he had been in the cave. It had only been a year, yet it felt like eternity. He sported a long beard. His hair was unkempt. He was dirty and disheveled. Old blood soaked his clothes. He hadn't changed, slept, gone to the bathroom, or done anything a human being needs to do to continue living. He was no longer a human. Victoria gave him a gift and he had learned to use it to his advantage.

Finally, after cutting off his head for the thousandth time, Varada, a beautiful, tall, blue-faced god appeared to him. He radiated a white aura, so bright it would blind a human. He looks down and sees Xander's decapitated head. Varada laughs and waves his hands. Xander gasps loudly, then looks around, dazed. He sees Varada and stumbles to his knees then bows his head, and Varada laughs again.

"Hello, my child, how can I help you? You've been asking for a boon," Varada said, the cave's walls shaking from the boom of his thundering voice.

"Umm... Uh... Umm... I would like to become invincible to gods, and all mythical beings!" Xander spurts out.

Varada laughs, "Oh, is that all? What will you do with this power?"

"Let's just say that I have a few loose ends that I need to tie up," Xander says.

"Alright, seems like fun! I will always be here, just ask if you need advice, but just know that there is always a price to pay for any gift." Varada boomed.

"So, that's it? You just say here you go, have some powers, there might be some fine print?" Xander inquires.

"Well, if you don't want them, I can take them back. However, once you sign this contract, no one can take them away." Varada says.

Varada snaps and a glowing golden contract appears out of thin air. Xander notices there is no pen to sign with. The words are written in a language he doesn't understand and a circle and some odd letters at the bottom of the contract.

"Do... do...you have a pen?" Xander stutters.

Varada laughs loudly, he cuts Xander's head off. Xander wakes up slumped in the corner of his bedroom. He frantically checks his pockets and his chest then feels his neck. He is in perfect health. He is in his room, not the cave. He stands up and walks over to his mirror. His face is clean-shaven. He is clean. He sees a beam of light peeking out from the curtains. The light burns his hand. He watches it sizzle for a moment then closes the curtains and runs to the mirror. He looks at his eyes. They change from red to black and back to red, again.

He opens his mouth and his fangs come out, but now he feels in complete control of them. Xander has never felt so much power coursing through his veins. He could feel the movement and vibrations of the Earth underneath him. There is a baby in the house across the street. The next-door neighbor has the TV on. He could hear, smell, taste, and sense everything within a twenty-mile radius.

He hears the heartbeats of people throughout the town. They were pounding in his ears like a band of drummers. All different beats and times, yet they made music for him. He laughed a sinister laugh. It made the walls of his apartment vibrate and shake. He sighed and looked at his arms. His veins were glowing red, pulsating in his arms. He no longer needed to physically drain his prey anymore. Now he could steal their lifeforce by tuning into their energy through the ether. Xander laughs again and feels the vibrations from his laughter reverberate through his body. A light radiates from his chest.

He feels tension pulling his chest with great force. He closes his eyes. Once he opens them, the pulling sensation stops. He is in the park. It is midday, which is bad news for him. He screams. His arms and back are sizzling in the sun's bright rays. He looks around in the park, realizing that this is the very spot where he threw Victoria and made her burn in the sun's rays.

He has a flashing memory. He sees her dancing with him in the clouded reality that he created. He sees himself dip her, kiss her deeply, and time slows. Then, time returns to normal. He throws her on the grass in the park. Her back sizzles. Her body is smoking all over. He feels her pain. He screams and closes his eyes. He opens them and finds he's back in his room again.

Xander is on his knees, the rug underneath him feels soft in his hands. His whole body is still smoking from the sun's rays, cooked from the exposure. He is a creature of darkness now and he could never stay in the sun again. He didn't mind. Even when he was human, he never cared for sunlight, so it wasn't much of a sacrifice for him.

He was a comedian for a local club but when he was changed by Victoria that didn't matter anymore. His dream was to be the next Louis C.K., but fate had a different path for him. He had known Victoria in many different lifetimes. And throughout them, he always loved her. This was a strong, ancient connection spanning centuries. How did it come to this?

Now she was with someone else. She moved on from her so-called "deep feelings" for Xander. He could feel her on the other side of the world from in his house. He could sense her in her castle. She was sleeping. Xander stood up off the dirty rug. He just stood there for a minute, wondering how he even ended up on the floor. Or how he never noticed how dirty the carpet was. But he shook these thoughts off and began his yoga routine. He lit the incense, did his first pose, and felt the power building in his chest. His chest was glowing, a beam of red light, glowing brighter and brighter with each passing second. He feels a pull from her and sees Victoria sleeping in her bed. She is snoring and her hair is a mess. Her makeup is smeared, and her shirt is placed in ways that are not flattering. Xander looks in disgust as he sees the monkey prince in her bed. He is shirtless and sleeping also. The whole room smells kind of like corn chips and raw sourdough bread.

"How can she want to be with this beast? How could she humiliate me like that? What did I ever do to deserve that?" Xander thought to himself. He looks around and realizes he is seeing all of this through the mirror in her room. The same mirror that once reflected himself in a suit, getting a haircut from Wilson. He was so familiar with the layout of her room that he could picture it in his mind's eye perfectly.

It looked the same as it did when they were together. The only difference now was that there was more hair everywhere from her monkey prince. "At least she looked happy," Xander thought.

That made Xander smile. He couldn't help but still feel that same spark he had felt when they had shared a magical kiss. He recalled that it was in the garden. The birds were singing. Their chorus grew into a crescendo. Time slowed. Their lips met and he was weightless. There was something about her that he just could not let go of. She cast him out of society and made him live his undead life on the lam. He had always wanted to be free. To live his life unaccountable. But nothing had worked out for him. He just couldn't catch a break.

Xander breathes in deeply and feels his spirit rejoin his body. His chest stops glowing, but his hands still have a dark purple aura. He walks to the incense, smothers the flame, then sits on his bed. He lies in his bed for the first time in what feels like an eternity. The pillow and the mattress are so soft, it's like sleeping on a cloud. The little things that once made him anxious no longer mattered. He had immense power. He closes his eyes and drifts off for the first time since he began a thousand self-beheadings. How many years was he in the cave? He no longer had a concept of time or material squabbles. The only thing he could see now was the finish line: an unyielding drive to bring revenge upon his creator, now his nemesis, Queen Victoria.

All he wanted in this world was devastation on her and her disgusting monkey beast. Xander had lived his life eating rats in a filthy cave, but he knew he would rather be a cave beast than some weird monkey guy. At least Xander could shower and wash the corn chip and piss smell down the drain.

He feels weightless as water hits his face. He senses all the grime falling off him. All the darkness and fear, washing down the drain. He felt like a new man, monster, or whatever he was.

He opens the curtain and rips each ring off the shower rod, one by one, sending them flying off with an amazing force. It took very little effort. He felt lighter, stronger, and surer of himself. For once in his life, he knew his place in the universe. He knew what he wanted. All he had to do was sit in the shadows and wait until the time was right to strike. Until then, the best way to hide from someone was in plain sight.

Xander walked from his bathtub to the mirror in his room, looking up and down at his reflection. He could see his aura. It had a navy blue hue, with little spots of green and brown to it. His eyes had turned blue, then he closed his eyes and concentrated. When opened his eyes, his hair was bleached blonde. He sighed, then laughed. He couldn't believe the incredible sensation of dominance over his fears and emotions, as well as the chemicals and atoms that made up his flesh.

He was drunk on his immense power. He felt dizzy but in a good way. He laughed. His house shook with the force of his laughter. He arrived at the comedy club he used to frequent. The sun set, and the lights had just turned on. There is a humming coming from them. He never noticed the powerful smell of piss radiating from the alley behind the club before. Xander opens the door, and a wave of body odor and misery attacks his nostrils.

"Failed dreams and disappointment... Why did I never notice this before?" He thought to himself. It's like the place hadn't changed, yet everything looked, felt, and smelled different.

He spots John in the corner; in the same booth he always hangs out in. He attempts to get John's attention, but he doesn't notice him. There is a skinny woman near him. She had many tattoos and is flat-chested with a bob haircut. She has freckles on her face. She sits next to a man with a mustache that makes him look like he's overcompensating for something.

He has his arm around her. He has salt and pepper hair and wears thick, black-framed glasses. The mustachioed man whispers something into her ear. Xander can hear their conversation, through all the noise in the club. He tunes into their words.

"Hey, do you think I should do the joke about all the butt stuff we've been experimenting with?" the man says. The skinny, freckled woman laughs.

Xander looks down at his feet. He can't see them. He realizes that no one else can see him either. He waves his hand in a person's face. They don't react to him. He looks at someone else. Xander's confused. "Why can't they see me?" He thought. He walks to the bathroom, making his way through the crowd. He pushes the door open. The bathroom is empty and smells like shit and bleach. He feels like he's going to vomit from how overwhelming the smell is.

He looks in the mirror. There is no reflection in it. He double takes, then waves at the mirror. "What the fuck?!" he says to himself.

He closes his eyes and concentrates. He opens his eyes again and now sees himself in the reflection. His eyes are blood-red and glowing. He closes them tightly, opens them, and they are brown. He looks up and down at himself. He nods in approval and exits the bathroom. The feedback from the microphone is so loud he covers his ears. It screeches with each bad joke and coffee-stained breath that assaults it.

He stands up straight and takes a deep breath. Time freezes. The comedian on stage is stuck in place. No one is laughing or drinking their beers. Xander stands in a yoga pose, breathing deeply and deliberately. Time speeds up and returns to normal. He walks up to the booth and slides in next to John. John turns to Xander and smiles.

"Hey man, long time no see, you look good, did you lose weight?" John says.

He grabs Xander's hand and hugs him.

"Nah, I've just been busy at work, so I haven't really had time to hang out at night. I get home and I'm beat, but I had some free time and I decided to come by," Xander says.

John stares at him, skeptically.

"I never noticed this, but are your eyes blue?" He inquires.

Xander pulls him into a half hug. "Don't worry about it. It's great seeing you, man! I just wanted to see how you're doing," Xander pulls away, his eyes have gone back to being brown.

"Ok, man, whatever you say! I'm just happy to see you. It's been so long…" John says, hesitantly.

"Is there a spot on the lineup for me to do a five?" Xander asks.

"Yeah, bro, I always save a spot for you," John says.

"Of course, you do. Who am I up after?" Xander looks down at John's notes.

"Granger is up next, then Kira. Then, you can go. They're both doing ten each," John says, referencing his notes on the table.

Xander looks deeply into John's eyes. "Listen, I need a loyal friend right now. Do you think you can be that for me? Loyal, above anything else. Would you endanger yourself if that is what it took to maintain your loyalty?" Xander asks.

"Sure, buddy," John says.

"Well, then I guess we have an accord. Let's shake on it," Xander says.

"Ok," John replies. He gladly shakes Xander's hand.

John feels a poke in his palm. "Ouch!" John yells.

"Sorry about that! I must have accidentally poked you with my ring. Here let me help you with that," Xander says.

He looks at John's palm. It is bleeding. Xander presses his palm against it and squeezes it. He moves his hand away and the wound is completely healed. John looks on in complete shock. He studies his hand thoroughly and can't believe his eyes.

What John didn't notice is that Xander cut his own hand and leaked some of his monstrous blood into the cut. Now John was infected. John felt his heart beating in his ears. The sound grows louder and louder until it gets so loud that he has to cover his ears.

John closes his eyes tightly and grabs his chest. His eyes glow a dark red hue. Xander laughs. John chokes and coughs. A moment later, his coughing turns into a sinister laugh. Xander stops time in the club. John looks around in awe.

"Whoa, did you practice magic while you were gone?" John asks.

Xander looks at him with pity, he is thrilled he has found a little puppy to follow him around and react to every whim.

"Yeah, something like that, alright, we need to do something. Suivez-moi," Xander says.

John follows intently. "Oui, Monsieur," John replies.

They scoot out of the booth and push their way through the densely packed crowd. Finally, they make their way to the door. John opens it and holds it open for Xander. He floats through it. John chuckles. He is not sure if what he's seeing is real and follows Xander closely.

Xander moves quickly, reaching the spot on the bench where he had killed his friend, Kevin. He touches the bloodstain from the spurting neck wound he had given him. Kevin was his first kill, and you never forget your first. Xander sees a flash of the memory that this spot's nostalgia holds for him. He sees himself bite Kevin and Kevin's body goes limp.

Then, he bites his arm and tries to shove it in Kevin's mouth. Kevin bubbles up and dissolves into a thick, gooey paste. Xander tries frantically to collect the goo, but it slips through his fingers. He yells and kicks a nearby tree as the goo disintegrates, then he flies off. John had just witnessed this entire memory. His mouth was hanging open in horrific realization.

"What the fuck, man, you killed Kevin! Then you dissolved him into a weird sludge?" John screams. "What kind of fucked up shit have you gotten yourself into, bro?" John says, breathing hard.

Xander slowly turns to him. He takes a deep breath. "This is why I brought you here, to prove your loyalty. If you'd like to end up like Kevin, I can arrange that. If not, you're going to help me bring him back," Xander says in a calm voice.

"Sure... sure, whatever you need, I'm here for it," John says in a shaky voice, too terrified of Xander to consider crossing him.

"Good, you've made the right choice. There is always a sacrifice when you bring someone back," Xander whispers.

Xander grabs John by the arm. He twists it as he looks him deeply in the eyes. He cuts off John's head with his freakishly long fingernails. He drops John's lifeless body on the ground, blood gushing out of his neck. Xander then touches the old blood stain left by Kevin. It begins to grow and bubble.

Kevin's body begins to re-emerge from the blood that is pooling together and growing larger. His head pops out, inflated like a balloon from the river of blood flowing together. There is a loud pop and then Kevin reappears altogether, as if nothing had ever happened. His eyes glow a dark red color just as John's do. Kevin looks down at his body and touches his chest. He feels his head, then jumps and cheers.

"I'm back bitches! Hey Xander, Why do ghosts take the elevator, it lifts their spirits. How do you stop a bull from charging? You cancel his credit card. Oh yeah, I still got it, man!" Kevin makes a whooping noise and raises his hand in the air. He does jumping jacks. He has never felt so energized like he just woke from a very, very, deep nap.

Xander waves his hands and John's head reattaches itself and his arm untwists. John takes a very deep breath. He touches his chest, still breathing heavily. Then he checks his head and his arms.

"Was I just fucking dead?" John squeals.

"No, don't worry about it, you're fine," Xander says in a cool voice. "Kevin, I thought you were dead too, how...what...Uh..." John stutters.

Kevin is dancing. It is very awkward and uncomfortable. He is, quite literally, dancing to the beat of his own drum.

Xander appears in front of John. "SSSSLLLLEEEEEEEPP," Xander hisses.

Everything fades to black. John wakes up gasping for air. He is back in the booth of the comedy club. The show is still going on. Granger is on stage telling jokes in the background. John looks around, thoroughly confused. Kevin is sitting in a booth near John, laughing and clapping for Granger. The noise from the club is muffled. The room is spinning. John can hear the heartbeats of everyone in the room. Xander is nowhere to be found. He looks around. Everyone claps for Granger as he bows and walks off the stage. Kevin walks onstage and takes the microphone.

"Hey everyone, how are you feeling?" Kevin shouts into the microphone. There is loud feedback from the microphone. The crowd cheers. Kevin smiles ominously as his eyes flash red. John looks around anxiously. It seems like nobody else even noticed.

"So, I had this girlfriend once..." Kevin continues. The crowd laughs. "Oh, come on, that wasn't even the punch line! Is it really that funny that I could have a partner who considers my advances to be consensual?" The crowd laughs again.

"Ok, fine, she said something that I wasn't sure if it was a compliment. She was a slam poet, so everything was overly dramatic with her. She also wrote songs. Not great songs, but she was kind of cute and down to do some dirty shit with me. Then one day, she played this song she wrote about how we ate a crunch wrap in her car and chugged white claws in the bathroom of the Olive Garden. I thought, Ok, that's weird, her songs sounded like she wrote them in high school. But then she hits me with some really weird lyrics. She says she loves the gap between my teeth, and that she wants her secrets to live there for eternity."

The crowd laughs, and Kevin makes a confused face.

"I didn't think my gap was that bad man, damn. Let's just say that I broke up with her the next day." The crowd roars. "All I'm saying is that no matter how hot someone is if she brags that she's taking medication for her issues, you should think twice before you stick your dick in crazy. Now there's nothing wrong with taking medication and getting therapy, but if that's how she introduces herself, run the other way, very fast. I feel like that's how Amber Heard and Captain Jack Sparrow met, she was like I'm Amber, I have to take my meds every hour or I can't stop lying." The crowd laughs again. The sound fades. The room is spinning as everything goes black.

John gasps for air. He wakes up in his bed. His dog's nose is at the end of the bed, watching him. John looks around. Everything seemed normal. Nothing was ever going to be normal again. The end was coming soon. John couldn't escape the deep sense of dread. His heart was pounding out of his chest. He was pouring sweat. Was that normal? What was normal? Normal was before. Normal could never be again.

CHAPTER 15

Some time had passed when Xander woke up next to someone who dressed like a teenager but was, in fact, an adult. She wore little footy pajamas, and her hair was in pigtails. Her name was Gabbi, she also loved Twilight. She had a fantasy of her being Bella and Xander was Satan, I mean Edward. It was a weird quirk that she had. She acted like a teenager, dressed like one, and listened to music that only little girls liked.

Xander thought it was charming, in a peculiar way, besides she had a lot to offer him in terms of him building an army. She had a lot of admirers online. A lot of people were willing to pay her a lot of money to dress like a teenager and call them daddy. It is a sick world, but the more idiots that are controlled by Xander the better. She had people who listened to her and paid her to do her ridiculous, histrionic poetry.

"They could be lured in by this slag, then I'll turn them and make them part of my undead militia." He thought.

After all, she had a nice car and a job. All Xander had to do was make her feel like she could always do better to please him, and she would be his devoted slave. It was too easy. He just had to sit back and let his devotees do all the work. If he had known how great being the leader of a cult was, he would've done it eons ago.

Now that Xander remembered all of his past lives, he obtained the wisdom of his past failures, he could conquer the world. He knew the key to his power was being the ruler of something much bigger. This dirt town he was forced to hide in was completely insignificant compared to the multitudes that he could rule over.

He knew he had to come up with a plan. Followers would be essential to winning the big war. He found solitude in waiting for the end. His mind was focused, and he could feel the energy rising, but Gabbi interjects with nonsense, constantly, and ruins his concentration.

"Monsieur, would you like a back rub?" Gabbi chirped from the corner.

Xander sighs and rolls his eyes, "Sure, hun," he says.

He gestures for her to approach him. She begins rubbing his neck. She was like an unlimited supply of energy, beaming with the rays of sunlight. He takes her hand, and gently he leads her around to the front of the chair he was sitting in. Then he brings her onto his lap. She smiles and puts her arms around his neck. They look into each other's eyes and smile. He breathes out and brings her head in close. He unexpectedly takes her head and rips it off. Then he drinks the fountain of blood, spraying from her gaping neck hole. He drops her body on the floor with no regard. She thumps on the ground. Her head is positioned near her severed torso and legs. Xander wipes his mouth on his sleeve and laughs.

He waves his hands. Gabbi's head is forced back onto her body. Her neck cracks in several places. Then, the blood on the floor absorbs back through her neck. She is standing behind the chair, in the same position she was before he tore her body in two. She cracks her neck, then goes back to massaging his neck. He laughs louder, and she smiles.

This is what he always wanted. It had finally come true. Yet, this would never be enough. He had to take back the control that he once had over Queenie. Then, he would take over her whole kingdom, the perfect foundation for his new empire.

He was no longer in the cave; he had seen the light, and now he could own the sun. Why would he stop at this stupid little town? He hated the sunlight, he had to remain in the shadows, but if owning the sun meant ultimate power, he was ready to get burned.

Gabbi finishes rubbing his neck and grabs her cell phone. She proceeds to take many selfies in different poses. Xander rolls his eyes. She is not a person to him. She was like a nuisance child, an obligation in an adult's body. She had a price tag. She used her online presence to fund her "music career". He looked at her with disdain and hate. Especially because at times, she reminded him of Victoria. No one could even compare to her. She was far superior to any modern, young being.

Victoria was sophisticated and wise. She was also thousands of years old. Gabbi's soul had never been turned before this lifetime, so she was thirty-something in human years. In Xander's eyes, she was a baby, despite being a fully mature adult human. But humans really were weak and pathetic. They were worms that needed beings like Xander to save them from only having one insignificant lifetime.

"Gabbi, come to me," Xander says.

He gestures to her but doesn't look her in the eye. She sits on his lap. He cradles her and pats her head.

"How would you like to live in a castle? Would you like to be a little princess?" Xander asks.

"Of course, I'd love to wear a tiara and prance around the garden in a huge castle," Gabbi giggles, then she swings her arms and imagines herself as a princess.

"You're going to help me with something," Xander says.

"Anything, Master," Gabbi replies eagerly.

Victoria is sucked back into her atrocious reality, Xander had his hands on her forehead and was forcing her to see these memories. She was in the dreadful cave. She could smell the brutal lifestyle that Xander was living in this shithole. Gabbi was lying on the floor. Her head was a few feet from her body. The floor of the cave was drenched in her blood. Queen Victoria waved her hands in the air. Her arms were shackled to a wall, but she was able to move them enough to put Gabbi back together. Her body was reformed to the state it had been before it was violently ripped in twain.

"I take it that he's done that to you a few times," Victoria says. She looks into Gabbi's eyes with pity.

"Done what?" Gabbi says, oblivious that Xander had ripped her head off to intimidate Victoria.

She made Xander. No matter what powers he had, the energy they used came from the collective. She knew him better than he knew himself. Victoria knew exactly where she was and how this would end. But right now, all she could do was take pity on the sad overgrown child sitting cross-legged in front of her, with her hair in a scrunchie and her loud accessories. This poor simple child, her soul was so young when she was turned. There was not enough darkness to change her or enough years for her mind to handle it. The process made her simple. She was already very weak-minded, now she was a complete dunce.

Xander still had trouble turning people into mystical beings. Victoria could only shake her head at this insipid, sweet, thirty-something, who acted sixteen. It was like he had taken her out of the oven too early, and now her brain wasn't fully cooked, the middle was still a bit mushy.

"Fucking amateur..." she thought to herself.

"Who's an amateur, Mistress?" Gabbi blurted out.

"Nothing sweetie, tell me about yourself, what's your name?" Victoria said in a mothering tone.

She glowed a bright pink hue. Gabbi curled up next to Victoria and rested her head on her stomach. Victoria positioned herself so that she could stroke her hair. Gabbi was humming to herself, a simple tune, her hair glowed as she sang.

"Oh wow, is that your thing? So, you're a healer." Victoria says.

Gabbi's hair glows brighter as she sings. Victoria absorbs the light through her hands. She flexes her hands, she loves the feeling of the energy coursing through her veins. Her hands glow with power. She breaks out of her chains and manages to support Gabbi's head on her lap. Victoria runs her fingers through Gabbi's hair. Gabbi stops humming, she looks up at Victoria, innocently.

"Did that help you, Mistress?" Gabbi asks.

"Yes, it did, thank you, ma douce," Victoria whispers.

Gabbi is shivering slightly. Victoria tears a large piece of fabric off of her dress then drapes it over Gabbi's shoulders and cradles her.

"Your soul is so youthful and energetic. I see why he keeps you around. He is using you; you know that?" Victoria asks.

"What do you mean, Mistress? He looks out for my best interests, that's what he told me," Gabbi says, yet she feels a sense of dread.

The sun was still high in the sky. There was no sunlight in the cave, no way of being antagonized by its mighty rays. The sun might not kill them, but it would make them vulnerable. Victoria was just grateful they had some shelter to shade them from it. She couldn't shake the feeling that this was only phase one of Xander's plan. What was he waiting for? Victoria couldn't read him as well as she could before. He made Gabbi sleep in the cave every day. When he woke up, once the sun went down, he would bring her out to feed on her then he would make her shiver in this filthy cave all day. Victoria was ancient and had lived through some brutal time periods herself. This reality was very cruel towards women throughout the ages.

Victoria was around at the beginning of this reality. As Gabbi slept, Victoria rubbed her arm to make sure she was warm. She ripped off another piece of fabric from her dress, she used it to guide Gabbi's head safely to the ground, then she waved her hand and created a feather bed for Gabbi.

She was in a warm bed, under a warm blanket, with many pillows and stuffed animals. She rolls over and snores. Victoria smiles, then she points at the shackles on her legs. They explode. Escaping her bonds was way too easy, there had to be more lying in wait.

Victoria waves her arms and creates a bubble around the mouth of the cave so that nothing can enter it and disturb Gabbi's much-needed slumber. Victoria goes to a deeper part of the cave. She floats so she can see every nook and cranny of the cave. It is pitch black to the human eye, but she could see things differently than Xander's little smooth-brained minions, or even Xander for that matter. There was a large hole in the middle of the floor in the cave. Victoria floated down into it with ease. The hole was much deeper than she initially thought. When would this end?

She finally sees the floor approach her feet. She braces for the landing, but it is surprisingly very soft and quite enjoyable. Even though her hair was a mess, and her dress was torn to shreds, she still had her dignity. She attempts to straighten her hair with her hands. She flattens what was left of her skirt. She sees a hidden tunnel to the right of her and follows it. It goes on for some time. There are many different scents, some flowery, others skunky, and faint hints of fruit. This is a strange place. It has no end in sight. Weird smells, but nothing else. Finally, there is a pinprick of light. Victoria makes sure her skin is covered so that she doesn't get burned. She is compelled to continue towards the light. It grows the closer she comes to it.

She emerges from a hole in the ceiling, doing her best to conceal her face from the sun. However, for some reason, the light does not affect her. She puts her hand in the rays of light. They don't burn her in the slightest. She looks up, skeptically. Then she sees a wooden floorboard with a small eye hole in it. She floats up to it and looks through.

She sees Svarga, but it looks different. Everything looks new, freshly built. She looks around. Rudra is standing above her. Maya is sitting in the chair near him. They look much younger and where was Jackson? This all seemed familiar, but Victoria wasn't sure why. Victoria floats back down to the base of the cave. She flies down the long hallway she came in from, and then she zooms toward Gabbi.

Gabbi is still fast asleep, sucking on her thumb and cuddling with a stuffed animal. Victoria smiles and chuckles.

"She's adorable. After all this is over, I might keep her as a pet," Victoria thinks.

Victoria walks in the darkness again. She comes across the spot where Xander would cut off his head and meditate. She can smell it, his blood painted the vicinity and soaked into every pore of the cave. It was caked with ooze, a thick layer of blood that filled the walls with the stench of raw steak and old pennies.

Victoria zoned in on the energy echo left behind by her dumb-shit ex. She followed his routine exactly. The yoga moves he would do for countless hours, she was able to see and feel everything he had experienced, in a matter of seconds. She could hear Jackson. He was sobbing. She worried about him. She felt a pressure in her chest then she cut off her head.

She didn't bleed a drop of blood, and yet her head came off with no effort. She used her claw nails to sever it from her body. It was like ripping wrapping paper off of a present on Christmas. It took no effort and the adrenaline made it even easier. She hears a whisper.

"Victoria," a voice that is so familiar says.

"What did you give him, Varada?" She asks.

He appears. The blue god is mighty in stature and towers over Victoria. He is extremely fit, his muscles have muscles on them. He has long, flowing, black hair, arranged in a bun on his head, and a great, long, black beard which compliments his piercing brown eyes.

Victoria is not intimidated by him at all. He wears a large belt, a flowy, thin, white shirt, and flowing, thin, yellow pants. He shrinks himself down to Victoria's size. She is not at all amused by this.

"What did you do, Varada?" She says in a stern tone.

"He cut off his head a thousand times and asked me for a teensy tiny boon," Varada says coyly.

"Varada, you didn't answer my question," Victoria says more forcefully, then grabs his beard. He winces in pain. "Tell me what you did, you, stupid, stupid fuck. I know you did something, otherwise he wouldn't have had the power to kidnap me." Victoria says in a quiet hiss at him.

Back at Victoria's castle, Jackson is sleeping on their bed. Rudra is standing in a doorway. He knocks. Jackson wraps himself in a tight blanket cocoon.

"Son, you slept for sixteen hours, how are you feeling?" Rudra says as he lightly touches his shoulder. Jackson shrugs and does not turn around.

"You have to get out of bed, kiddo. You can't sleep and sulk anymore. We have a plan," Rudra says.

Jackson sits up and looks at his father. His eyes are puffy, and his fur is in disarray. Rudra hugs Jackson.

"It's going to be ok son, we'll get her back, I promise," Rudra says, patting his back.

"I just can't live without her dad, what am I going to do if this doesn't work?" Jackson says between sniffles.

"It will work. We've dealt with more shit than this, and so has Vic. She's tough, she can take care of herself. She will be ok," Rudra says, wiping Jackson's tears.

CHAPTER 16

Jackson made his way to the kitchen. He has a blanket wrapped around his head and body like a jacket. He is shirtless and wearing some very ratty pajama pants. Wilson was tugging at his torn and matted pant leg. He was like an innocent, sweet, little puppy and he adored Jackson. He would follow him to the ends of the Earth. Wilson never really cared for Xander. He was always rude and treated him like a bug he wanted to squish.

"Master Jack, may I make you a cuppa?" Wilson squeaks.

"Merci, non, ma douce, I can make a cuppa tea for myself, I'm not completely helpless." Jackson chuckles at Wilson, he is so tiny compared to him and so naive.

"Please Master, Mistress wouldn't want you to make tea for yourself. She would be upset and ask why she keeps me if I can't even be a good host and serve tea to the Master." Wilson wheezes as he breathes.

"In this hypothetical situation, would she kick you across the room and laugh?" Jackson says with a smile.

"Yes Master, but it always made her feel better to hurt me. On really bad days she would murder me. I always deserved it though and she would always bring me back. Fit as a fiddle, no pain or anything. She's so good to me, I miss her so much, Master. Excuse my emotional outburst." Wilson cries with little, tiny wheezes and squeaks between gasps of air.

Jackson picks Wilson up and puts him on his shoulder, then he pats his leg.

"It's ok, buddy, we'll get her back, I miss her too. We'll make this tea together, how about that? It will be our secret, okay?" Jackson says, comforting the poor, pathetic creature.

Wilson nods, and then in a flash, the tea kettle is on the stove, and the burner is on high. A teacup and saucer are placed on the counter, next to the stove. Another flash, then there is a fabric napkin and a teaspoon, Wilson appears in front of Jackson.

"What flavor of tea would you like, Master?" Wilson wheezes.

"Whoa little guy, don't hurt yourself," Jackson says.

"How about some kind of herbal tea, and you know how I like it. I'll be in the library, can you bring two more setups, my dad and Moccus are in there. I have to talk with them, I can't keep moping and feeling sorry for myself. That's not what mon coeur would want me to do," Jackson said, solemnly.

"Yes, of course, Master, whatever you desire," Wilson squeaks. Jackson pats his head and turns to enter the hallway.

Jackson walks down the hallway. He is plagued with memories of Victoria. Her scent still lingers. She has saturated herself in every nook and cranny of this place.

Jackson's thoughts begin to overwhelm him. There is a loud ringing in his ears. His body begins to heat up. There is light radiating out of his eyes. He tries to close his eyes in an attempt to control his anger, but he fails. He closes his eyes very tightly, hoping that it will just stop. He feels a small tug on his pants and looks down. The ringing has stopped and the lights in his eyes have subsided.

"Hello Wilson, how can I help you?" Jackson says to him.

Wilson calms down.

"Master, the tea is in the library for you, just how you like it with a splash of agave and milk. Master Moccus requested that I escort you there if you need it, master," Wheezes Wilson.

"Ok, you can ride on my shoulder if you want," Jackson says with a laugh.

Wilson jumps up and down in excitement. Jackson picks Wilson up and places him with ease. They continue down the hallway. Wilson lets out a tiny, "WHEEEE," noise as they float down the large hallway, toward the east staircase.

They pass the ballroom, the bathroom, and the dressing room that they spent most of their days in. She had only been gone for a few days, but it felt like a lifetime without having that warm comforting presence next to him when he was sleeping.

She would glow bright pink and radiate a warm light when she was having a good dream. She would roll over and kiss his head every morning. Then she would refuse to get up. They could live in those three rooms for the rest of eternity and never get tired of it. Now that she is gone, the only thing left in this castle is a cold emptiness that she left with her absence.

Many different types of mythical beings were bustling through the halls. There are more than enough rooms in the castle to fit an entire army comfortably. Even with all of the commotion in the castle, there was still an emptiness that hung in the air. The ballroom was filled to the brim with some of the universe's most powerful and oldest beings. Now it was dusty and filled with cobwebs, a mere memory of what it was.

He remembers how amazing she looked the night that he proposed to her, and how he kicked Xander's sorry ass. It was a magical night. It will never be recreated and now it means nothing because the one being that mattered the most in the entire cosmos is gone. How could Jackson function without her bossing him around and making decisions for him?

He hadn't showered for a week. He barely ate. If it was possible to die of a broken heart, he was dying slowly from it. If anything happened to her, he wouldn't be able to go on. What is the point of living without her? Jackson enters the library. He lands on the ground and cracks the wooden floor. He sets Wilson on the ground gently. Wilson tugs at his pant leg again.

"Master Jack, are you alright? I have to gather the staff to make dinner for our many guests. Do you need any more assistance?" Wilson squeaks and wheezes.

"No, Wilson, thank you, that will be all," Jackson says.

"Ring this bell if you need me, I'll hear and I'll answer, anything for you Master Jack," Wilson says.

Wilson hands Jackson a silver bell with a seashell on the handle. He shakes and he gives a very unsteady bow, then he disappears in a flash. Jackson turns to his father and Moccus. They are huddled around a large table in the middle of the many shelves that were stuffed with every book ever written. Victoria loved to read and through the years she made a point to purchase every book that had ever been published. The first book that had ever been created on Earth was published in eight hundred sixty-eight or so. Victoria had books that were older than that, books that she had only obtained because she was old and able to move through different realities with ease.

She was friends with different beings that lived on different planets, in different galaxies. She was fascinated by the different cultures and frequencies that they resonated with.

Some of the books moved and flew by themselves. Some were made out of a material that couldn't be perceived by mortal beings. Her collection went on for miles. When Victoria did something she did it bigger than any normal being.

Jackson found a comfortable chair near the table so that he could listen to the plan his father had. He had fought by his father's side in every battle. He had never led an army to battle. He was lost and couldn't find his way. Normally he would just ask Vic what she thought. She would smack him and tell him to read her mind. Then, if he didn't get it, she would head butt his face until he got the message. It was a fun game they played. Jackson missed all of the yelling at him she did. She didn't yell because she was mad or abusive, she just had a big personality and not everyone could handle her being so over the top all the time.

Jackson loved that about her. She was never cool, always at least warm, if not bubbling over. It was part of her charm. If she called you names and yelled at you, that meant she cared very deeply for you. If she didn't make eye contact and rolled her eyes at every word you utter, you should run. She's probably going to kill you.

"Veera is on his way. He should be here any minute," Moccus says to Rudra.

Rudra turns to Jackson "Son, how are you holding up? Do you need anything?" Rudra hands Jackson a cup of tea, on a saucer, with a cloth napkin. Jackson takes it and sips it.

"Thanks, I needed that, I'm okay dad, I need to work on getting her back, what's your plan?" Jackson says as he sips his
"We just received intel that's not good. We have a solution, but you're really not going to like it." Moccus interjects.

"Just tell me what the plan is, I don't care if I'm going to like it or not, I need to get my fiancé back," Jackson breaks the teacup and tenses up as he speaks.

"We had to call Veera," Moccus blurts out.

"You called that clown? He's all air, water, and no brains. He's a joke! We might as well leave her to fend for herself. She'll be better off than having Veera try to save her."

Jackson stands and throws his saucer and napkin on the ground. It shatters everywhere, and then he pulls out the bell and rings it once. Before the echo of the bell has finished, Wilson is standing next to Jackson and looking up at him.

"How can I serve you and the other Masters?" Wilson squeaks. He looks down and sees the mess, he shakes his head and picks up the napkin.

"I'm really sorry, little man, I didn't mean to make a mess," Jackson says as he kneels to talk to him, at eye level.

"No problem, Master, I live to serve you. Mistress made much bigger messes when she would get angry. I miss cleaning up after her. I don't know what to do with all the idle time I spend not waiting on her hand and foot." Wilson wheezes.

He zooms away and comes back in less than a second. He is holding a broom and dustpan and cleans it up, disposing of the trash and getting rid of the broom in less than a second. He looks up at Jackson.

"May I get you another cuppa, Master?" Wilson squeaks at him.

"No, thank you, that won't be necessary," Jackson says as he pats his head.

Wilson smiles a disgusting, brown toothy grin. There are some spaces where there used to be teeth, and the teeth that are still there are brown and stained. It is a disgusting sight, but Jackson is amused by this odd creature. Jackson waves his hands to dismiss him.

"Dinner will be served in twenty minutes, Master. I can bring everyone a plate if you would take it in here. Just ring the bell if you need me, I'll be back with your plates," Wilson wheezes.

Jackson pats his head again.

"Ok, thank you, I'll take that tea with dinner, the minty one this time, please," Jackson says.

"Of course, Master," Wilson squeaks.

Jackson turns to Moccus and Rudra. They have been conversing about Veera while standing over a large table. It has a war map with many pieces on it. The pieces move on their own. As Rudra discusses the plans, the soldiers move and battle on their own.

"So, what exactly is that pompous idiot going to do to save my fiancé?" Jackson asks reluctantly.

"Well, that's the part you're going to be upset about. During our nightly meditation, we discovered something. Varada came to us and told us something unsettling," Moccus explains.

"Well, spit it out, what did he say?" Jackson says, losing his temper.

His eyes light up, just for a second. He moves toward Moccus. Rudra puts his hand on Jackson's chest and pushes him back.

"What he's trying to say is that Varada gave Xander a boon that makes him invincible to Gods, mythical beings, and demons. We can't kill him so easily. If you just barge in there, you're going to get hurt. Varada also thinks Xander may have figured out a way to get rid of us, permanently," Rudra says, in a stern voice.

"How? I thought that wasn't possible. You, ma, and Vic are all ancient ones, how are you vulnerable to that scum?" Jackson says in disbelief.
"I literally kicked his ass in five minutes with one hand behind my back. He's not that amazing, I honestly don't even know why Vic wasted her time creating him and dating him. She said she found a picture on his phone. It was a woman, and she was squatting over a plate and there was spaghetti involved…" Jackson is cut off by Rudra.

"We don't have time for that right now," Rudra interrupts.

"No, please continue. I was getting into your story. I think we have a minute to discuss the sick shit that humans enjoy," Moccus says sarcastically.

A voice startles all three of them, from behind their huddle. Veera is standing next to the table, Rudra and Moccus walk over to him and hug him. Jackson rolls his eyes and scoffs. They have a long history. Jackson takes the bell out of his pants pocket and rings it. Wilson appears.

Jackson whispers in Wilson's ear. Then he reappears holding a tray with two teacups. They are sitting on a saucer, with a napkin and a teaspoon on each set. There is also a plate that has tea biscuits with flowers on them. Jackson nods and pats Wilson on the head. Jackson takes the cup of tea on the right side, then he takes a tea biscuit. He dunks it in the tea and eats it sloppily. Wilson walks over to Veera and offers the tray to him.

"Oh, wow, full service! I feel very welcome, thank you. What is this thing?" Veera gestures to Wilson, confused.

Jackson walks over to Veera.

"Veera, this is Wilson. He is the house goblin, I guess. That's what you are, right, buddy?" Jackson asks Wilson and smiles.

"Yes, Master, I never really thought about it, but if that's what you think I am, then I guess that's what I am. I would consider myself more of a house butler," Wilson wheezes.

"Ha, he's hilarious, like a little talking dog. Is this a prank? Good one," Veera laughs hysterically.

Jackson nods at the door as he pats Wilson's head. Then Wilson nods back and zooms off.

"Ha, look at the little guy go, he's so fast," Veera says.

Veera is bent over laughing and holding his sides. He composes himself, wipes his eyes, and gets back to business.

"Sorry, that little guy was amazing, I want ten! I'll pay whatever you want, I need that little guy around my palace," Veera says.

Rudra and Moccus laughed with him and patted him on the back.

"So, what exactly is the plan here? I feel like you guys weren't really clear in your message. I mean, I got the email, but I'm still not sure what my role in this shit show is," Veera says. Rudra and Moccus burst out into uproarious laughter. They pat his back.

"Well, we need you to go into the cave and kill Xander," Moccus says, still laughing.

Veera straightens up and gets serious.

"Wait, what?" Veera asks, concerned.

"Yeah, you're such a great warrior. You can take him no problem, right?" Jackson chimes in from the corner of the table. He didn't want to be near Veera. He couldn't stand his musk of cedar and peppermint. He was so fake, he was wearing makeup and he had plastic surgery.

"Well, of course, I am a great warrior, but I'm no god like you guys, and I'm certainly not a demigod, like baby Jack over here. What do you need me for?" Veera says.

"You have the spirit that we need. The reason we need you is because you're not like us. Varada gave a boon to Xander. Now he is invincible to our powers, and we are no match for him. He is holding Victoria captive. So, we were thinking that there could be a loophole. Maybe we can't kill him, but you can," Moccus explains.

"How am I just going to waltz in there and kill him? Maybe I'll listen to his stand-up until I pass out from boredom. I looked up his social media profile. His stand-up routine is sad. It also said he's dating this chick who is a social media star." Veera pulls out his phone and shows them a video of Gabbi singing off-key.

"She is awful, someone should tell her to just give up. She can't carry a tune in a bucket, it's really sad. The reason she has so many followers is because of the way she dresses, not any talent to speak of. I mean, slam poetry? Come on..." Veera says.

Moccus, Rudram, and Veera laugh uproariously.

"Holy shit, I think you just figured it out, you're a genius, Veera," Jackson says.

He hugs him and picks him up off the ground, his back pops loudly.

"Jack, you're crushing my spine," Veera says, struggling to breathe.

Jackson sets him down and brushes off his shirt. Jackson had bits of biscuit crumbs in his face and fur and had just gotten it all over Veera's shoulder.

"Sorry about that man, I just got kind of excited, and I forget my own strength sometimes. I'm just anxious to get my fiancé home, I really miss her," Jackson says.

Veera nods in approval, "I'm still impressed man, I thought when you got down on one knee that she was going to punch you in the face and tell you to fuck yourself. I mean, she's pretty spicy. She's never said yes to anyone else," Veera says.

"Yeah, that's what she does every other time I ask her to marry me. Now I just do it to annoy her... did it..." Jackson trails off and tears up.

"Hey, I may be all show and no substance, I'm the first one to admit that, but I normally just close my eyes and hope something falls out of the sky to save me. It has worked one hundred percent of the times that I have tried it. My power is luck. I was born as an incarnation of Vishnu, and he does everything for me. I'm more privileged than Paris Hilton," Veera says.

"I really hate you," Jackson sighs and sniffles. They both laugh and hug.

"I know. I'm here for you, mon frere. I will close my eyes and shoot an arrow at his heart. There's no way I'll miss, then he'll die. You and Queenie can go back to hanging from the ceiling. That was legendary! I posted about it yesterday and got fifty likes," said Veera.

"I can't believe you're our only hope. Awesome, I'm living my worst nightmare. How did you get the video of me hanging from the ceiling?" Jackson says. He hangs his head. He lets go of the hug.

"Let's just say I was impressed, I shared it and I laughed my ass off. Check it out," Veera shows him a video on his phone of Victoria and Jackson having sex. He is hanging from the ceiling upside down and Victoria is riding him. She is screaming uncontrollably and he is making loud monkey screech noises. Jackson blushes and puts his head in his hands.

"Tell me about the good memories, how did you meet her? I'd love to find someone half as amazing as her," Veera says.

"It was an app called MonsterMash. She saw me and swiped right. Of course, I swiped right for her. She invited me over and we just clicked. She messaged me and asked why I was single and what I was doing on a hookup app. She told me she knew who I was right away. I felt it the moment I met her. She's amazing, like a ball of lightning, extremely unstable, but with immense power and beauty. She invented class and poise, literally," Jackson says.

He notices that Veera is ignoring him and staring at his phone. He rolls his eyes and walks out of the library then rings his bell. Wilson appears in a flash.

"Yes, Master?" Wilson wheezes.

"Bring my tea and my food to my room, please. I can't deal with anyone right now. I need some time alone," Jackson says, in a somber tone.

"Anything for you, Master," Wilson says before zooming off.

Jackson arrived in the room. It was hollow and dark. The sun was up outside. It was noonish. It was abnormal for him at this time. Victoria was a night owl and he had learned to enjoy the nighttime. Without her, the days were vast, hollow darkness, nothing.

The sun brought no comfort either. Without her, there was no joy, no happiness. She gave his life purpose and direction. Without her, he was just some arm candy, himbo, daddy's little rich boy.

Victoria loved him for who he was. He didn't need to be anyone else around her. They didn't know each other until they met on a dating app, but he knew of her. He felt like he had always known her. His dad would tell stories of the many battles that she helped them win. She's a goddess, everyone knows who she is. The humans have built temples for her, she was truly unique. Why was Xander keeping her alive? What was his goal?

Could he actually kill her? Xander couldn't even kill a deer with a hunting rifle, so why was there fear in his father's eyes? He had never seen his father afraid of anything. Now he was afraid that they might not get her back alive. If he kills the goddess, she'll take this entire reality with her. She was a spicy pepper bomb, and Xander's finger was on the detonator.

CHAPTER 17

Victoria hadn't had a good night's sleep since she had been in the cave. She had a nightly ritual in this cave. She would tell a story to Gabbi, put her to sleep, then create a bed for her. She would meditate and do yoga in the cave until she sensed Xander approaching. She tied her filthy, tattered dress into pant legs. She had it around her legs so that she had more mobility in the cave. She couldn't just leave the cave, though. The only thing holding her there was the fact that if she left, Xander would go after Jackson.

He knew that if he hurt Jackson, she would freak out, turn into her primal form, and destroy the universe. She had many forms that she could easily change into. Some forms were less stable than others and she couldn't release the infinite energy brewing inside her unless she suffered a great loss, such as her true love or the love of a child.

Since she had no children, Jackson would be the key to releasing her vital spirit. Time would restart and this existence as they knew it would cease to exist. It's already happened a few times, and it will happen again. That is just the cycle: life is created, then destroyed, over and over for all of eternity. Fate always has a way of finding its place. If this was the time it was meant to happen, then so be it. Unfortunately, for Xander, Rudra enjoyed living this life way too much to start over again, fate had other plans.

Victoria was doing a Tai Chi routine as Xander had done in the cave to channel the flow of the ether and his essence. Her eyes were closed, and she was deep in her mind. She had the flow of the universe at her fingertips. She danced and moved with the waves pulsating through her body. It was a mere shell to contain the vastness inside her.

She hears a noise and swiftly turns one hundred and eighty degrees. Veera appeared in the cave, startling her. She turned and he just appeared out of nowhere and it shocked her. She knew everything in the universe, or so she thought.

"Who the fuck are you? You look familiar, but I don't care enough about most mortals to know who they are. How did you get in here?" Victoria says, gasping in shock.

"You know what's weird, I have no idea how I got here. I was getting drunk with my buddy, Rudra and he wanted to see what my power was. I closed my eyes, chanted to myself, then I opened my eyes. All of a sudden, I was watching your sweet ass moves," Veera says coyly.

"Who are you?" You look a lot like Bhavah, but he's an ancient one and you're just a flimsy meat sack," Victoria says.

"No, that's not my name. I'm Veera. That's short for Veerarama. I'm sure you've heard of me," Veera says, then he smiles.

"No, I don't think I've heard of you. Should I have?" Victoria is confused.

"Really? My family has a temple dedicated to you, in the middle of our town. I have devoted my life to the goddess. Now the gods have given me a mission to come rescue you because they don't think they can do it without causing some kind of world-ending event. So they sent me." Veera says, slurring and stumbling. He hiccups loudly, Victoria sighs in frustration.

"Great, this is so just classic Rudra, fucking everything up and then calling me when it's gotten too far. I'm going to have to kill him myself aren't I?" Victoria's eyes glow red.

She emits a red light from her whole body. The cave is pitch black and the only light that is illuminating the cave is the aura around her.

"You're like an angry glow stick! How do you do that? That's cool, I wish I could do that. My power is stupid. I didn't earn it, though. I was born with it," Veera slurs.

Veera is drunk, not only on booze, the feeling was being magnified by the aura pulsating out of Victoria. Sandalwood and rose water, it was intoxicating. He swayed and couldn't find his balance. He leaned on the cave for support. She grabbed him and sped to the front of the cave. Gabbi was sleeping on a few ratty pieces of fabric. Queen Victoria had only created an illusion of a warm pink featherbed to make the cave bearable for her. The cave minimized Victoria's powers.

This was by design. This was a cave of punishment for beings who had lost a trial and had to be contained for the good of the rest of the universe. They used to house the Titans here. They are all now dead.
This cave called to Xander, and he got stuck in it. You can enter, but it is significantly harder to leave the cave. The ancient ones came together, during their Greek deity phase. They made up every god in every mythology. They changed forms, for the humans who served them.

There were eight ancient ones in total. They were all paired off and they could change their entire identity, but they always had the same spirit. The cave didn't show up on any human map, nor was there any mortal map that shows its existence. The cave entrance is hidden from anyone who isn't supposed to be there. Xander had turned that ancient magic on its head. He recently remembered that he was one of the eight. He used that to his advantage and now Victoria is stuck in this prison that he was supposed to be stuck in, with a drunk mortal no less.

"How am I supposed to hide you? Xander will sense you," Victoria whispers.

"Don't worry about it. I'll just take this sexy lady with me. We'll leave the way I came in and everything will work out," he says slurring and swaying.

He picks her up and walks unsteadily with her.

"That's not all she is, you fucking moron, that's Gabbi," Victoria sighs in frustration.

"No way, that's Gabbi Ricci? I love her, she's so tiny IRL," Veera snorts when he laughs, it echoes through the cave.

"You're not that much bigger than her," Victoria whispers.

She senses that the sun will be setting soon. She turns to the lower part of the cave, to see if there's anything to hide Veera with.

"Hey, Queenie, is there anything you want me to tell your man? Monkey, Guy?" Veera stumbles as he shouts this, she turns to him.

"Tell him I love him and I'm going to find my way to him. What makes you think we're getting out of this cave anytime soon? The sun is going down and Xander is coming in here to torture his poor, half-cooked servant. My servant gets treated with some dignity. This poor child has been given some powers, but she has some brain damage. She thinks she's sixteen and that her life is a music video. The poor dear is so simple. My heart aches for her," Victoria says.

She rubs Gabbi's head and looks down at her lovingly.

Victoria zooms to the other side of the cave. She looks desperately for something to conceal her intruder with. She didn't want him to deal with Xander's wrath. He was a human. After all, she had quite a fondness for humans. She thought they were cute, like puppies or kittens. She zoomed back up to the mouth of the cave, where she left Gabbi and Veera. He was harmless, he couldn't even stand up straight, what could he possibly do to hurt himself or Gabbi? Victoria looks down, shocked They are gone. Either he figured out how to hide or Xander discovered them. There is only one piece of torn fabric on the ground of the cave.

"Oh no. No, please no, not Gabbi, she's so innocent. Veera?! I hope they are unharmed," Victoria says to herself.

She looks around for them in a fury. She annihilates everything that she can get her hands on.

She cries, falling to the ground in defeat. She ties herself to the cave walls with the chains that Xander thinks hold her. The sun comes down, and Xander approaches the cave. He walks over to Victoria then he looks frantically for Gabbi. Victoria pretends to be asleep. Xander kicks her.

"Where is she?" Xander growls.

He moves close to Victoria's face and he grabs her neck.

"I helped her get free of you. I told her how to get out of the cave," Victoria says, gasping for air.

He picks her up off the ground by her throat and squeezes. He throws her. She hits the cave wall and bounces off, then lands on the ground. She is coughing and gasping for air.

"You're lying! I'll figure out how she got out, then I'll go straight for your precious Jack's throat. I know how to kill him and maybe I will. I want you to watch. I want you to see the light go out of his eyes," Xander growls.

"Oh, just do it, if you're going to already. I'm bored of your idle threats, pussy," Victoria spits at him.

He picks her up by her throat again.

"That's exactly what you want, isn't it? For me to go charging in blind, then your man-monkey beats my ass, turns me mortal, and makes me live my days as a human," Xander yells in her face. He drops her and floats with his back to her.

"Then I don't get to come back again. No, thank you! I'm enjoying the power I have right now and I'm not giving it up this time. We've done this tango countless times, Siddha. You always do this to me. I'm not falling for it this time. How low are you that you had to use my servant? I don't care about her at all. I'm not falling for it. Tell stupid Jack to kill her for all I care," Xander growls.

He floats towards the entrance of the cave.

"I'm going to get off tonight thinking about watching you sweat, Isaac. You've already fallen for whatever they have brewing for you," Victoria yells defiantly.

Victoria makes a triangle movement with her hands. A gust of wind comes out of her hands in the shape of a triangle. He doesn't look back at her. The gust of wind hits him, he flies into the mouth of the cave so hard that it causes a rumble in the walls. He gets up and dusts himself off nonchalantly, he leaves Victoria in the cave alone: no light, no friends, no Jackson, nothingness. Victoria sits cross-legged.

She puts her hands in prayer position on her heart chakra. There is a bright, green light radiating from her chest. Xander goes back to his room and begins his Tai Chi routine. He is channeling Victoria. His focus is only on her and her thoughts, everything she sees, he sees.

Meanwhile, Veera appears on a coffee table in the middle of a room. A few soldiers gathered around the TV. They were fighting over which show to watch on the TV. They stop fighting to stare at Veera, confused and skeptical.

"Holy shit, that was amazing. Not exactly how I planned, but that works," Veera says, breathless.

He hops down from the table he is standing on, still holding Gabbi. He runs down the hallway. She is still fast asleep, sucking her thumb and wrapped in a tattered piece of brown cloth. She's short and thin, even for a normal human. Veera was also slightly bigger than most humans. She was so cute and petite that he had to take her. It felt like capturing the flag. It's a fun game to him, and he has no idea how much danger his life is in.

Veera sets Gabbi down on a couch in a vacant room. He continues running until he sees Jackson sitting on a chair, holding a brush that Wilson used on Victoria's hair. He is crying, softly. Veera runs by his room, he backs up and approaches him, breathing heavily.

"Jack, bro, I talked to your boo," Veera says, trying to catch his breath.

"What do you mean?" Jackson looks up, sniffling and confused.

"Bro, I captured the flag, I know how these things go. They took your boo, I took his boo, then we have a boo off," Veera says breathlessly.

He gestures to Gabbi, in the other room.

"Stop saying boo, what the fuck are you talking about?" Jackson says forcefully, his eyes light up for a second. Veera puts his hands up, defensively.

"No disrespect, I talked to your old lady. She said she loves you and… and… umm… something else. I don't remember, it's not important. It was like kissy, kiss, kiss, touch me where it tickles, then she just called me a fucking moron and threatened to hit me," Veera blurts out.

Jackson nods.

"Yeah, that sounds like Vic. So, what do you mean you captured the flag?" Jackson sighs.

"I mean I took his boo! Look in this room. This is his bottom bitch, you know his main hoe?" Veera asks.

He points to the room across the hall. Jackson sees her on the couch, asleep. He looks skeptically at her. She is very small. Jackson rings his bell. Wilson appears.

"Yes, master?" Wilson responds to the bell.

"Take this tiny creature, thing. She's so little. Make her comfortable," Jackson says.

Gabbi was about five feet three inches, which is relatively average for a woman her age. Jackson was just massive and had no idea. Many confused mortals had seen Jackson in the woods and thought he was bigfoot. He hated that they always forgot his tail though in the depictions of him. Jackson grabs Veera's shoulder, pinching it.

"So, what happened after I left the room?" Jackson says through his teeth.

"Rudra busted out some really weird wine, he said he got it from a friend named Barkus or something like that," Veera slurs, then burps loudly.

"Anyway, it had some kind of weird flower or herbal ingredient. Well, it made me feel like I was stoned or something, it was amazing. Then Moccus and your dad put their thumbs on my forehead. They said some weird chant and then I ended up in the cave," Veera puts his hands on his knees and breathes deeply.

"I think I'm going to puke, I drank too much, and the energy your girl was putting out enhanced it. I was tripping balls," Veera grabs a trashcan and vomits violently.

"You saw Vic, how did you get out of the cave? The Titans were locked in there and couldn't get out. You can't even stand straight and you're tiny compared to Xander. He used to be like you too, but his height grew with his power," Jackson said with a sigh.

"Well, I'm not that much taller than Gabbi if you're saying our height difference is weird. I think it's cute. She's pocket-sized."

Veera picks his head up out of the trash and wipes his face with his sleeve. He puts the trash can on the floor with more effort than he intended.

"Was she ok? How did she look? Did she mention me?" Jackson screams in his face and shakes Veera.

"Stop shaking me, you're hurting me. She wouldn't shut up about you, that's what I said before. Kissy, kissy, whatever, I don't care. I'm getting sleepy," Veera whines.

Veera smacks his lips together then his eyes close. He passes out in Jackson's arms. Jackson sets Veera on the couch that Gabbi is sleeping on. Jackson flies down the hall, faster than he's ever moved before. He knocks on Moccus' door. It is locked and he is fast asleep. Jackson knocks insistently. Moccus opens the door, his eyes are half open and he is wearing a male nightgown.

"Where's the fire?" Moccus asks, sleepily.

"Get dad up. It's time. Veera just captured the flag." Jackson whispers urgently.

Moccus's eyes widen.

"Already? Damn, that was quick," Moccus yells in response to the shock.

CHAPTER 18

All of the billionaires that run this garbage, dirt planet are either ancient ones disguised as humans or are controlled by the ancients. Steve Jobs created Apple as a way to control the population. He knew that if you put sparkling lights in front of the simple humans, they would be easily amused. If they were amused, they would readily give their privacy away. Mark Zuckerberg is obviously not a human. He didn't even try to fake it.

Some people believe in crazy fringe beliefs. Then there are those who are especially touched and particularly brain dead, such as the QANON cult. Those guys are hilarious. The cult was started because of the twins. They made a bet on who could get the humans to believe in the craziest things. Estelle got them so riled up that they trampled each other to death. She convinced them to march on the capital and take over the government. The same year, they repealed Roe V. Wade. The country was already on the brink of civil war, but this was just hilarious to Estelle and Wolfgang.

The leftist, "politically correct" culture was equally insane. The red and the blue were two sides of the same fucked-up coin. The side of the coin that won the toss was in power at the time. The red color won more often because of all the fake news and recounting. So they said. Women deserve equal rights. All people deserve equal opportunities, and fighting for that is praiseworthy. Canceling someone because they said something on Instagram, however, is going way overboard.

The twins were pissing themselves watching the humans squabble over what words they could or could not say in public. Neither side would ever win, no matter who yelled the loudest. The gay community and straight community hated each other with equal prejudice. The PETA vegans used violence against humans to advocate for nonviolence against animals. The resurgence of anti-semitism was in full swing. Humans are ninety-nine percent genetically identical, there's no logical reason any of them should have as much conflict amongst themselves as they do.

There are whole groups of people who hate others because of the color of their skin. Women of color get it the worst. No one deserves the cruelty that this particular group has endured through the ages. This world was upside down. The Satanists are the ones fighting for equality and decent treatment for everyone. The Catholic priests are the ones touching little boys in the altar room. Then, they cover it up and get tax breaks for their church activities.

Wolfgang and Estelle caused all of this disarray. For the universe to have balance, there has to be light, but darkness also exists. Lighting the world on fire was like playing a chaotic Sims game. It meant nothing to them. They particularly enjoyed the cruelty and oppression that world leaders had inflicted on the masses. Estelle shape-shifted in the nineteen forties and got the German people all worked up about the Jewish population, then started a world war over it. Wolfgang thought that was a barrel of laughs. Wolfgang was FDR.

The resurgence of fascism was surprising to Estelle and Wolfgang. They didn't plan that, but when most of these towns are inbreeding, education goes out the window. Although fascist, Trump wasn't an ancient one, himself. His creepy goblin advisor Giuliani definitely was, though. His motley disguise hardly convinced anybody that he was a real person.

Wolfgang didn't have to try that hard to convince people that he was a great leader. It didn't matter, if it was a bad game, they could just change their identities, start a cult, and begin anew. There was no shortage of idiots in every village.

The ancient ones had no gender or race. They were all formless, timeless things, all realities at all times. A human's head would explode if they tried to comprehend the vastness of their existence. They had to look like a human for humans to understand them. They had no nationality or stake in anyone's war or conflict unless they created it out of boredom. To them, it was a game that repeated over and over for eternity. They were just dressing up to pass the time and disrupt the grating noise of the eternal ennui. The universe would get destroyed, it would be reborn, then a few Jeremy Bearimies later, it would be destroyed again. The creatures they created on the planet would grow and evolve, then they would blow it up and start a new game.

This was the cycle, but Xander was bored of it. He was trying to upset the natural order and this time the conflict did indeed involve them. Now he was the king of the comedy club, just like he had always dreamed in his mortal life. It was a lonely existence, high up on this pedestal that he had built for himself.

Most eternal beings were able to shape-shift. Even though the humans were much smaller than the ancient ones, they could disguise themselves to walk amongst them. Humans were tiny and their brains weren't able to comprehend the necessary perception of their true essence. Humans were too easy to manipulate and control.

Xander entered the club looking like his original human form, how he looked before Victoria brought him back in this body. It was like wearing a zip-up costume, he would simply snap his fingers then he would transform into a frail meat sack, a poop and fluid factory. He was three feet shorter but still had the same mind. The more he meditated and cut his head off the taller he got. He was a god amongst men, and they had no idea. He was just Xander to them. He had only changed a few of his cronies. The rest of the humans could not perceive how much he was draining them.

Gabbi was someone whom he quite enjoyed. She was simple and sweet. She thought she was a good singer, he humored her because she had a large following online. Somehow people seemed to actually like her and her music. To be fair, the humans were simple small-brained ape people. They were amused by sparkly screens that played five-second videos of someone moving glitter around in a bowl. This world started out interesting, but this age of man was sad, soft, fat, and feeble. They were easy to exploit, and quick to anger. Creating outrage was easy. All you had to do was say something that offended one person. As long as the offended person had a following or friends on the internet they could create public outrage.

Gabbi did this many times on her social media platforms. She would post a video about her feelings and people would care about it. She didn't like the way a fast food worker looked at her, so she posted a video online of her having feelings about it. Then another video of that fast food chain having sent her an apology letter. She opened the letter on camera, with her address and name fully visible for her many followers to see. There were some exceptional people, people who didn't live their lives on their phones. Some people take selfies of their new haircuts, or with their shitty boyfriends, who rolled their eyes when they spoke.

Gabbi was supposed to perform at the club that night, but unfortunately, she was gone and Xander didn't care enough about her to charge headfirst into an obvious trap. Instead, he walked into the club with Queen Victoria. She had shackles on her wrists and ankles, but they were invisible to the humans. He had made her take a shower and put a new dress on. She was wearing a fabulous dark-purple dress with loud hair accessories. It was much shorter and much more revealing than she was used to wearing, but Xander forced her to look like Gabbi and perform in her place. Victoria changed her appearance to look like Gabbi, but anyone who wasn't human could see her true face.

Victoria held Xander's hand, smiled, and acted the part. She was good at hiding in plain sight. She was also an amazing actress and chameleon. She always made a point to keep up with the language of the humans. She was fascinated by them and studied their cultures, so she fit in seamlessly. The club was packed to the brim with people, but Xander did not doubt that she could perform for the crowd. She was amazing in the spotlight. Xander pokes her and prompts her to move using telepathy. She leans in and kisses him, the crowd cheers, he feels that spark that is still present.

"I broke my vows for you and I have done it over and over. I will never stop loving you. I made a mistake choosing Tara, I'm trying to fix this reality so that we can finally be together, instead of you and that fucking monkey," Xander says to her telepathically.

"You broke your vows for someone who doesn't feel the same and all you've ever done is lie and manipulate your way to the top. You don't love me, you don't even know what love is. You told that astrologer to lie to me, no one made you do that. Since the beginning of time, all you have done is lie, cheat, and steal. The only thing you care about is yourself. That's what it's always been about, what you want," she responds.

He leans in and kisses her again, the crowd roars again.

"You're not allowed to leave me this time, I won't let you," he whispers in her ear.

They both bow to the crowd and smile.

He signed a contract saying that no matter the circumstances, he could never kill her. It didn't say anything about torturing or enslaving her. He poked her hard with an invisible finger, so hard she fell backstage. She struggles to stand, clears her throat, then continues to the dressing room area. The shackles limited her powers, so she had to pick and choose what she used them for, or there could be some dangerous consequences. If she somehow glitched out, she could reveal her true form and destroy the club. Xander was counting on that.

He was also counting on his enemies to infiltrate this show. He made Victoria put out a video with a coded message and send it to Jackson's phone. The trap was set. He knew they would do something, just like they always did in this eternal chess match they played with each other. Inevitably someone would get mad and flip the table. That's when they would make it the humans' problem. It was Helen of Troy all over again.

Victoria is thrown around backstage by Xander. She falls on the floor and scrapes her knees. She doesn't look up. Instead, she is looking at the dirty tile she landed on. She cries quietly to herself. She sniffles and hears a familiar voice.

"Don't cry queenie, we're here to save you. Toco la mano," He whispers.

Victoria looks up. Veera is standing above her, holding his hand out. She grabs it and he helps her stand up.

"Wow, I never thought I'd say this, but I might not take you back to Jack. You look just like Gabbi, but like, with your face. I'm not going to lie; I have a full chub for this look," Veera says, undressing her with his eyes. Victoria slaps him, he grabs his face in pain.

"Damn, queenie, it was a joke, if you can take a monkey penis, you can take a joke," Veera says, holding his face.

She slaps him again.

"I don't have time to give you a lesson in manners and how to be respectful to a lady. Also, don't threaten to keep me away from my man. I will literally destroy you. We can't talk here, Xander could be listening," She looks around suspiciously.

"No, Rudra already took care of that. We're playing chess or something. I don't know. I never listen to what they have to say. They just give me good food and wine that tastes like Italian herbs, then they chant around me, and here I am," Veera slurs.

"Are you drunk? How are you here to save me?! Are you going to annoy me to death? Do you even have a plan?" Victoria would scream if she wasn't trying to whisper.

"No, they didn't tell me anything. They just gave me the wine, then asked me if I could host a comedy show and I was like 'Sure, why not, this place is boring and sad anyway. Everyone's always wandering around crying about how much we miss Victoria. Wah, wah, wah, get my fiancé back, she's the goddess, we need to save her. Blah blah blah.' It's so boring, I'm over it. I welcomed leaving that stinking monkey zoo," Veera whined.

Victoria's anger turns to a smile. Then she hugs Veera so hard that it cracks his back. She releases him and he hits the ground. She picks him up and dusts him off.

"Checkmate," she says.

She places her thumbs on his forehead, there is a loud humming noise. The room is vibrating, the walls are pulsating from the vibrations of the humming, and Veera sees a bright light. The lights go down in the club, there is silence in the audience. Xander has heard the humming. It is faint, but he nods at John and Kevin to go check it out.

His favorite booth is on a small platform in the very back row. There were two huge TVs on each side of the stage. He had recently eaten the owner of this club and made his own VIP section. If anyone sat there was not approved by Xander, they would be killed and turned into a mindless zombie. That's how he made most of his army. People came from all over the world to this club. They would be drawn to his throne. They would sit down in his chair, and it would swallow them. They would return as zombie slaves to do his bidding and fight his war. Gabbi was special. She was one of the first ones he turned. He tried to bring back Sofie, but her body was destroyed by Victoria. So, he bit her instead and made her this smooth-brained simple girl.

She reminded him to appreciate the small things, such as Disney movies and dancing at inappropriate times, like when they were watching

Law and Order. There was no dance beat in that song, but she was dancing to the beat of her own drum. She would ask him stupid questions like, "Do you think Jesus' hair was greasy?" He would just look at her and pat her head. When he was in his human disguise, they would be at the club together and he would be posing as her boyfriend. It never felt right to him. He would kiss her and do other fun things, but beyond that, he hated her voice. The things she said and the pitch she said them in were grating on his ears. In her mind, they were dating. She was a high school drama teacher in a small town. He was her master and creator. They were not equal in his mind. It had been the same with Wilson.

Victoria found herself missing Wilson. Most of all she missed Jack, but she also loved Wilson. She didn't fetishize him like Xander did Gabbi, but she loved him like a purse dog.

Veera walks onstage, into the spotlight. "Good evening, I'm Veera, short for Veerarama. You don't know who I am, that's cool. I'm new to town, but I know you all so well because I have the shades of lipstick from all of your moms on my dick. That's right, I fucked all of your moms!" Veera yells into the microphone.

The crowd roars with laughter.

"Well, some of them just blew me," he continued. John and Kevin surprise Victoria from behind, backstage. Their eyes are glowing red, and they are staring, expressionless at her.

"What was that humming noise?" Kevin asks.

Victoria gasps. She didn't hear him sneak upon her.

"It was nothing, that human was nervous, so I showed him how to meditate and control his nerves. I must have been chanting too loud," Victoria says with a shaky voice.

Xander appears behind her.

"Are they in the club, Vic?" Xander hisses in her ear. She shudders in disgust. Her skin crawls when his breath hits her neck.

"What are you talking about? Who? I've been standing backstage the whole time. I was talking to the new host. Now he's killing it. I just gave him a boost of confidence," Victoria insists.

Xander seems suspicious, but he believes her.

"No funny business, I'm not playing."
Xander, Kevin, and John disappear.

Victoria collapses on the floor and cries in her hands. She dries her tears and stands up. She straightens her tiny, pleather skirt and wipes her face with her hand. Then she takes a deep breath and readies herself for her one-woman show. Gabbi had named it "Big Feelings". Victoria was about to have to pretend to be a smooth-brained, slag. Gabbi's show was just a compilation of her ridiculous social media songs and poems. Even if she tried, she could never be like these simpletons. She was special. There had been many wars over her, she had tall poppy syndrome. She was going to have to put on the show of her long life. She knew they had a plan and she just had to have faith.

CHAPTER 19

Victoria would poke her head out of the curtain once in a while to watch the performers on stage. They were all extremely mediocre, but it didn't matter anyway. This town is where failed performers go to die. Performing stand-up in this tiny dirt town, in this shitty club, meant they had all given up on a real stand-up career. The only reason people showed up tonight is because Xander brought something they wanted to see. It was a guest celebrity stand-up comedian. He was some social media clown or something. Victoria had no idea who he was. He was an insignificant roadblock, in the way of getting back to Jack.

Before she knew it, it was her turn on the stage. Veera announced her and the lights went black. She walks onto the stage and takes the microphone. She sings a song that she makes up on the spot. She does a whole routine that lasts about forty-five minutes. It is amazing. Everyone is buzzing about how Gabbi's music is better all of a sudden.

Gabbi had been performing the same three songs on stage for the last four or five years. She didn't even write one of the songs that she performed on stage, but she would call it her prayer. It was a cover of a pop song that led into a poem she wrote. One of the lines was that she "scrolled the bible of Instagram makeup tutorials". It was utter jibber-jabber, designed to entice the easily entertained masses. Mostly, she just had to wear low-cut shirts, and high-cut shorts, and shake herself around on the camera. That's what got her all those followers. Not her "musical talent".
Male humans were interested in women who strip for the camera and pretend to be deep. The second that a man would make a rude comment or slut-shame her she would post about it, and that would give her even more

media attention. Many men were looking up her skirts in photos. That's all it took to be an influencer.

This performance was different. Victoria could sing beautifully, in key, and she refused to perform slam poetry. Slam poetry was a way of expressing how you feel in the loudest and most annoying way possible. Sometimes they would just put words together and hope they sounded deep. "We ate a crunch wrap in my car, then slammed some white claws in the Olive Garden bathroom." That was a lyric from one of Gabbi's songs. Victoria was a sophisticated goddess. She didn't understand any of Gabbi's music, and she didn't know what a crunch wrap or a white claw was. She had never heard of Taylor Swift or Carly Jepson.

Somehow, she convinced the crowd that they were the same person. The crowd was so enticed by all the shiny bobbles on her head, neck, and arms. She could have stood on stage and sang I'm A Little Teapot for fifteen minutes and they would have had the same reaction. These people were simple, even for humans. Most of the male comedians that got onstage talked about their penises and the women talked about their vaginas. The crowd was aching for anything that seemed remotely entertaining or creative.

The lights went out in the middle of Victoria's set. She looked around and noticed that all of the humans were frozen in time. She stands up, panicking.

She calls into the darkness, "Jack... Jack, is that you?"

Victoria is shaking. Her powers are still limited because of the shackles. The lights come back up and the show continues. Time resumes as it was before. Victoria finishes her set, then she stands and bows. She exits the stage. There is a standing ovation for her. The walls shake with how hard the crowd is cheering.

"Thanks for coming out tonight, have a good night," Veera says from backstage into the microphone. The thunderous applause continues for quite some time. It fades, and the people in the audience talk amongst themselves. Xander holds the door open and thanks all of the humans for coming as they exit. Xander locks the door and turns around. The only ones left in the club are Veera and Victoria, dressed as Gabbi.

Xander approaches them in an intimidating manner. They are talking and laughing. He turns to Veera.

"Hey man, that was great. I've never met you, what happened to the other host?" Xander hisses as he shakes his hand.

"He ate some bad eggs or something, it was coming out both ends, it was really explosive," Veera responds.

He pulls away from his handshake.

"No, I mean who approved this? I have to approve of anyone who goes on my stage. I've never seen you," Xander says more aggressively.

"Umm, well about that," Veera says, as he pulls a glass jar from his back pocket.

It contains some kind of gray dust. He throws it on the ground. It shatters, sending the dust flying everywhere. Xander covers his eyes and coughs from a large smoke cloud that has filled the club. When the smoke clears and the dust has settled, Victoria and Veera have disappeared. Xander looks around furiously. He screams and bangs his hands on the tile, he breaks the floor. A broom falls from the other end of the stage room, he hears Victoria and Veera arguing about it. He zooms over to them. They are attempting to break her shackles. Veera struggles to get them off. They stop when they realize Xander is behind them. Veera yipes, then Xander picks Veera up off the ground by his neck. In a flash, Veera jabs Xander in the eye with his thumb. Xander drops Veera and claps a hand over his eye.

"Ow, what the fuck!?" Xander screams.

Victoria had managed to get one of her hands out of her shackles and force-pushed Xander into the wall. She rushes over to Veera, picks him up with her free hand, and attempts to run away with him on her shoulder. As Victoria reaches for the door to exit, Xander stands up and pulls her back with his mind. She flies back with great force. She repositions Veera, so that when the blow hits she lands on the ground, he is covered by her arm and is not hurt. She takes the impact from hitting the ground.

"This was your big escape attempt? This is so sad. They're not even coming for you. Look around Queenie, you're all alone," Xander yells in a demonic voice. He laughs evilly.

He feels a tap on his shoulder, he looks behind him. It is Jackson.

"Are you sure about that?" Jackson says as he punches him into the wall.

"Jack!" Victoria screams.

She makes sure Veera is ok, then she runs to Jackson and kisses him. She leaps in his arms. Jackson tries to fly out of the door with her, but as he does, Victoria flies out of his arms and is thrown violently onto the stage. It crumbles on top of her, and she is knocked out cold. Jackson rushes to her side. She can't leave the club as long as she is still shackled. She had only managed to get one hand and one foot free. Jackson picks up her head, but she is completely limp. By the time Jackson turns around, his army of monkey warriors has already surrounded the building. Rudra had entered the building and Moccus was standing behind him.

Just then, shadows appear out of nowhere. They turn into people Xander had turned into mindless zombies. Rudra gives a vocal signal, and the two armies battle each other. The monkeys are tearing the zombies limb from limb. These zombie creatures had no chance. Xander sees his army being decimated. He doesn't care. They were always supposed to be human shields for him anyway. He zoomed over to Victoria's unconscious body. He picks her up and teleports her to the cave. He drops her hard on the floor of the cave. She wakes up and winces in pain. She still only has two limbs free from her bindings.

"You're going to pay for this, Queenie Weenie. I'm going to kill that stupid, smelly monkey man!" Xander huffs and puffs at her.

A voice at the mouth of the cave shouts, "Now!" An arrow comes flying through the cave and hits Xander in the back. He wails in pain. His back begins to dissolve. He rips out the arrow in an attempt to stop the disintegration. He pants heavily. Jackson and Veera enter the cave.

"You want the chance to kill me? I'm standing right here. Are we going to dance? I'm done with this foreplay. Let's do this, for real," Jackson rips off his shirt and starts doing Capoeira steps.

Veera is holding a bow-and-arrow. His arrow is knocked and pointed at Xander. Veera takes a step back and trips. The arrow goes flying wild but bounces off a stalactite and lands right in Xander's eye. Xander rips it out violently. His eye has completely dissolved. He shrieks in pain. Victoria zooms to Veera and takes his bow and arrows. She knocks an arrow and shoots it at Xander's heart, it bounces off and makes no impact. She looks down at the bow in confusion. Then she realizes that no eternal beings can kill him, but Veera is a human. Xander rips off his shirt and begins mirroring

Jackson's Capoeira moves. Xander kicks Jackson in the face. Jackson kicks in his direction, but Xander dodges it.

Veera hit his head when he fell and is presently knocked out cold, on the ground. Victoria slaps his face, trying to wake him up. He doesn't wake back up. She tries desperately. Nothing. She can't just leave her man to die in this cave, but she needs to get help.

She wiggles her other arm out of the restraint, then she gestures in the direction of the comedy club, which is a few miles away from the cave.

"You could join me, Mahakala. We could rule the world together," Xander says while they are kicking around each other.

"I'm not going to become that. We need this world to thrive. You know that, Isaac. Why are you trying to upset the natural order? We used to be friends until you stole Vic. Why Xander? Why?" Jackson yells. They continue kicking and punching each other.

"Why do we need order when chaos is so much more fun? Fuck this place, I'm done with your order and rules. I want to play by my own rules. I love her too," Xander growls.

"It doesn't have to be like this, mon frere, we used to be great together," Jackson yells.

"You made your choice a long time ago when you chose Ram in the war of the Bhagavad Gita. We're not brothers, we're not even friends! I want her! I love her! You can't be my friend if you're with her!" Xander yells.

He pulls a blade out of thin air and stabs Jackson in the stomach. Victoria screams a blood-curdling scream. It echoes, reverbing down the block. The armies that are fighting hear the scream back at the club. The zombies turn into smoke and disappear. Rudra's army looks around in confusion and anticipation. Back in the cave, Xander has fled the scene. Victoria finally managed to get free from her shackles. She is holding Jackson and Veera, crying. She picks them up and positions herself near the mouth of the cave.

There is a barrier, so that you can come in, but you can't leave, no matter how powerful you are. Victoria summons all the rage that she felt about her man being hurt. She repositions Veera and puts him on her other shoulder. She summons all her might and screams. It bursts through the bubble that was holding her in the cave. She had done something a crew of other ancient beings couldn't do, but she was devastated. Her havoc could make the whole universe pop like the bubble in the cave. She flies to her castle and lands at the entrance. She whistles loudly, and Wilson and Gabbi appear.

"Mistress, you are a sight for sore eyes. Are you alright, did he hurt you, Mistress? You're bleeding. What are you wearing, Mistress?" Wilson asks with a confused look at her outfit.

"Hurry, I need you to take Jack and Veera, they are hurt pretty badly. I'm fine, please help Jack." She sniffles. Wilson takes them and returns faster than the speed of light. Wilson picks Victoria up and places her in the bed next to Jackson. Home again, it felt good, but not like this. Was Jackson going to live?

Moccus and Rudra stumble into the room behind them. Victoria is curled up in the fetal position in the bed next to Jackson. Jackson is unconscious and roughly bandaged. He is not in good shape. Victoria is crying. Rudra grabs Jackson's hand. Moccus helps Victoria out of the bed.

"Come with me, Queenie, you need your rest," Moccus says.

Moccus attempts to lead her by her hand. She resists. He hugs her and picks her up, then he carries her out of the room, she throws her arms around him and sobs into his shoulder. He pats her back sympathetically and takes her to another room. The troops arrive back at the castle and slowly the walls fill with soldiers. Wilson helps Victoria into a warm bubble bath. There is soft classical music in the background. She sits in the bathtub, leaning her head to one side, sobbing hysterically.

"I'm so glad you're back, Mistress. I kept up the castle and I was a good host to all of the guests," Wilson wheezes.

"Thank you, Wilson," she says quietly, through her tears.

"He's going to be alright, Mistress. Master Jack is very strong! He looked how you do now when You were gone. He'll be alright. You two are back together, nothing else matters now," Wilson says, trying to cheer her up.

"Oh, stop trying to make me feel better. What if he never recovers? All of this will have been for nothing," she sobs.

"He got you back, Mistress, that's something. Would you like a cuppa ma'am? I'll get you some fruit tea and a biscuit if you'd like?" Wilson asks, trying to cheer her up.

"I just wanted to be with Jackson. That's all I thought about when I was in the cave. Now he's hurt and it's all my fault," Victoria cries.

"It's not your fault, mistress. He would have done anything to save you. He was incomplete without you," Wilson says.

"Xander said he would do it. I thought he was just bluffing. He told me he had the blade of eternity," Victoria sobs and screams.
"Master Jack will be ok, I promise. That's not going to kill him. Nothing can kill him, or you," Wilson says.

He zooms away and comes back with a saucer of tea. He places it on the counter next to the sink. Wilson helps her out of the bathtub. The sun began to rise. Victoria is getting ready for bed. Jackson begins to stir. Victoria rushes to his side and grabs hold of his hand.

"W-Who's there? Vic, is that you?" Jackson says, still groggy, opening his eyes.

"Yes, Jack, it's me! Oh, babe, I'm so happy you're alright," Victoria says.

Jackson opens his eyes. He looks around. He's in the cave. Xander is holding his hand. Jackson yelps. He sits up, quickly and aggressively grabs Victoria's throat. He chokes her, forcefully. She grabs his arm.

"It's... me... you... dumbass," Victoria struggles to say, she hits his arm.

Rudra sees the commotion and runs in. He grabs Jackson's wrist and frees Victoria. She breathes deeply and coughs. Jackson force pushes his dad into the wall. Victoria uses her powers to knock him back out. Jackson falls back asleep on the pillow. She puts a green bubble around him. He is peaceful and has pleasant dreams.

"Rudra, the blade has corrupted him. He thought I was Xander and that he was still in the cave," Victoria bursts into tears. She coughs and gags.

"He's gone Rudra, he's gone," she screams and sobs. She collapses to her knees. Rudra picks her up and holds her. She throws her arms around his massive neck and cries into his shoulder.

"We'll get him back, don't worry. I'll take you to Moccus. He'll know what to do," Rudra says. He pats her back and comforts her, she cries uncontrollably.

He carries her in his arms, he flies down the large corridors. She is surprisingly light for having so much power. How can this sweet fragile woman wield more power than the entirety of everyone else in this castle? They arrive at Moccus' door. He is asleep. They knock loudly. He opens the door. His eyes are halfway open.

"Why does everyone in this castle hate sleep?" Moccus asks grumpily.

"Moccus, the blade of eternity has corrupted Jack's mind. We need your help. It made him attack Queenie," Rudra says urgently.

"UGH! Why can't you ever wake me up because it was someone's birthday, and I didn't get a piece of cake yet? It's always this shit with you guys." Moccus says and he sighs loudly. "Has anyone checked on the human hero?" Moccus asks, frustrated.

"I was just doing a last check before I went to bed. Maya takes the day shift most of the time and she was already sleeping. I went to Veera's room, he was still asleep, he's fine. Then I heard a commotion from Jack's room, and I saw him holding Queenie up by her neck," Rudra says.

"Great, this is fuckin' great! So, I guess our plan completely blew up in our faces then?" Moccus says, now at his wit's end.

Victoria bursts into tears and cries into Rudra's shoulder.

"I'm going to put Queenie to bed, then I'll come get you," Rudra whispers.

"I think that's a good idea," Moccus says.

He leaves, slamming the door in Rudra's face. Rudra flies to an unoccupied room. He lays her in the bed there and tucks her in. She is crying hysterically.

"I'll be right back," Rudra says.

He comes back quickly with his wife. She sits in the chair next to the bed. She holds Victoria's hand. She sobs loudly. Maya strokes her hand and shushes her.

"It's ok, I'm here. Jack is going to be ok. Rudra won't let anything happen to our son. He would do anything for Jack and you. That's why they went to save you. You're a part of this family and we have each other's backs," Maya says, comfortingly.

Victoria rolls over and sobs, Maya rubs her back and shushes her. Victoria calms down and falls asleep. Maya leaves the room and puts a protective pink bubble around it. She whistles. Two monkey guards appear in front of her. She looks them in the eyes.

"No one goes in, and no one disturbs her. She needs to sleep. She's been through a lot. You got it?" She asks the guards.

They nod and stand on either side of the door.

Jackson is in Svarga. Victoria is there with him, she is sitting in a chair, on the porch. She is crying, he hears her sobbing loudly. He runs to her and tries to comfort her, but there is a green bubble preventing him from being near her. He bangs on the bubble, but she doesn't hear him. He hears a familiar hissing noise in the distance and turns around. He has to get out, he has to be with Victoria, he can do nothing, but dream of her.

CHAPTER 20

A week after the whole ordeal, Jackson still hadn't woken up. He was essentially in a magic coma. In his dreams, he was in the cave with Xander, battling it out to the death. Every time Jackson would strike, Xander would parry. Xander was always a step ahead of Jackson. Jackson realized that he had underestimated Xander. He had grown much more powerful since the last time they fought.

Victoria wandered the halls, wailing loudly. She had become a phantom of her former self. She was a banshee haunting the halls. She was pale as a ghost. She barely slept, she never ate, and she didn't care how she looked. She always cared about her appearance, even when she was in the cave. The thought that Jackson could come rescue her with her looking like a mess was a nightmare to her. Today was very different. She wore a robe, a thin nightgown, and fuzzy red slippers. She refused to take care of herself. She couldn't do anything without him.

She never left his room. She would wait outside the door day and night. Wilson had done his best to cheer her up and serve her, but there was no cheer for her to draw from. There was only darkness, at least in the cave there was some hope. All she thought about was getting out to get back to him. Now that it has become a reality, it felt empty without him. His laughter normally boomed through the castle.

His charm was contagious. You just couldn't be in a bad mood with him. He was such a warm, hairy beam of sunlight.

Not knowing whether or not he was going to live sucked all of the warmth and light from Victoria. Moccus and Rudra worked day and night to wake him up. They had stopped the poison from spreading through his body, but it had already corrupted his mind. They used Victoria's power to stop the poison in his throat. It was a thin bandage on a huge gash. They had to find a way to bring him back. There just had to be something they were missing. They had tried meditating over him for a few days. They were able to enter his mind and see his hallucinations.

They could only helplessly watch as he was bested over and over again by Xander. They didn't want Queenie to be in the room. She was in no condition to help, and they were afraid he would try to hurt her again. She was too fragile and couldn't take the emotional pain of losing him. They had to keep her calm and stable or she could go off and take everything with her.

Maya never left her side. She held her and cradled her. All Victoria could do was sob. Maya was equally worried about her precious prince, her baby boy, but she had to be strong for Victoria. Maya, Rudra, and Queenie had known each other since the beginning. They felt like they owed her, in a way. Countless battles seemed desolate, but then Queenie would come in and save the day at the last moment. Most of the time, that meant blowing everything up and starting over, but not every time. Jackson had only been born a few hundred years ago. She had never known him before, but now the thought of him being gone left a black cloud of sorrow throughout the whole castle.

Rudra and Maya were ancient ones. They were the second ones to pair off. They were always together, no matter what. Queenie had a harder time with her partner. She was with her partner from the beginning, and she was happy. She never felt like she made the wrong choice until Xander decided that he wasn't satisfied with his partner and the long droning movement of time. He had always admired Victoria and one day, he came to her and asked if she wanted to help with something.

Isaac convinced her to follow him to a garden he was working on. He was attempting to make a new race of apes, but they had no hair and were a little bit more civilized. Victoria was compelled by this idea for the garden. She and Xander watched them day and night. Then one night something unexpected happened. She and Xander realized they had feelings for each other and that they had for some time. They were caught mid-coitus by the people he had created. Eve had stumbled onto them. She couldn't comprehend what she saw, so Xander made her think she was talking to a snake and eating an apple.

Then Rudra punished her for eating the apple and thus began an age of sexism and misogyny. This dimension began with an eternal crime being committed. You were not allowed to step out on your partner and if you did, there would be consequences.

They did what they could to cover it up, but eventually, they were caught in the act by Xander's partner, Tara. She told the other five ancients.

There was a trial and Xander was found guilty. He was forced to remain in a human's body for a few lifetimes to learn his lesson.

Victoria was forced to live on the Earth, wandering until she could find the other half that she had betrayed.

Jackson was the other soul that completed her. She had hooked up a few times with Xander in his various human lifetimes, but Victoria had become quite lonely. There was one lifetime when all four of them were given a test. Of course, Xander manipulated the situation and blew it all up. That was his signature move. Victoria tried to bring Xander's memories back and also his powers, but he hadn't evolved enough to handle it, in his human meat-sack form. The first time she tried, he melted and turned into goo, then dissolved into the dirt.

This planet was horrible. The whole world was run on corruption and greed. It was not easy to thrive when you were born to a family of vagrants, living on the fringe of society. That happened to him many times, living a life of poverty. What kind of soul are you when there is no help, everyone hates you and you have to live your life eating scraps the people with money left in the garbage can? Eating cave rats wasn't that odd, most of his lifetimes he was dwelling in tunnels under the city streets and in the slums.

Victoria didn't have to reincarnate, she just existed for many millennia, wandering the Earth, searching for the love she threw away on a whim. She could shapeshift and convince the humans that she was one of them. They loved her, but she had to feed on them or she would get weak.

Xander was always manipulative, a gas lighter, and always played the victim. Especially if everything was his fault. He had a perfectly lovely partner, but he could never just be happy with what he had. He always thought he could do better and have more. In this lifetime, his partner was Adam. He knew as soon as he saw him at the engagement party. It was like a magnet. He couldn't ignore it, but he still loved Victoria deeply.

Rudra and Maya decided that they wanted to experience life on Earth, just not living among the filthy, tiny humans. They started their own society deep in a valley, protected by magic so that humans couldn't just stumble upon their village. They thrived there for millennia. They had kept in contact and kept a close eye on Victoria. They never judged her or condemned her for what she did with Xander. They had always been close. Out of all the ancients, these three were always together. They founded their society to be close to her.

Jackson was the physical manifestation of Victoria's eternal partner. He had been given a blessing at conception. Varada came down to a monkey woman in their village. She had prayed for a child. She had no partner and wanted a baby. Varada came down and gave her a seed. She planted it in her garden. She watered it and made sure it thrived. One morning, she came into her garden and discovered a baby monkey, where the plant should have been. He was covered in dirt and crying. She wrapped the baby in her apron and shushed him. He had fallen asleep in a hammock, she set up in her garden, so she could keep an eye on him.

Even though he was a God, he was still a tiny baby. He woke up early from his nap and was hungry. He looked up at the sky."That peach looks delicious," he thought. Mistaking the sun for a peach, he flew towards it. The king of the sky, Indra saw a random flying object and struck him with lightning. Jackson fell to the Earth, he was dead. Varada was not happy, so Indra made a deal with him. He could bring his son back, but he wouldn't have any memories of him being a God.

Then the villager, who had planted him in her garden, brought him to Maya and Rudra and told them everything. They thought it would be better if he lived with the king and queen. They invited the villager to live with them, in their castle, and she accepted. Her name was Aditi. She would be Jackson's live-in nanny and he would learn to control his powers from daily lessons with Moccus. Aditi would make him breakfast, then he would go to school just like all of the other children in the village.

This was a village with tons of different animal types. There were cats, monkeys and elephants. All the animals who lived there stood on two legs and walked upright. They all had the same language, they never treated Jackson like he was different. They accepted and admired him. He had the spirit of the god, but he was still just a monkey. He would come home from school, and Aditi would fix him an afternoon snack. Then, Sugriva, the village guru, would give him Tai Chi lessons in the courtyard. Jackson was not the kind of child who needed extra help. Jackson went straight from crawling to flying. He wanted to master the universe in one day. Sugriva taught him how to control his impulses and powers.

There was no way to teach him how to come back from being stabbed with the blade of eternity. This blade was forged after a great battle. All of the beings who fought laid down their weapons, to incite peace and end the fighting. All of the weapons were melted down and turned into one blade that represents all of the violence and conflict in the world. Forged by Agni, the god of fire, and sealed in a deep tomb hidden from everyone, even the ancients.

The blade was guarded by two ancients, playing an infinite game of backgammon. The only way to get it would be to bribe the guards, break in, or kill them. They guarded it because all of the ancients agreed that this was too much power and violence for anyone to wield. They sealed it in an impenetrable vault. The only way to reach the vault was by going deep into the Earth. You had to go through several layers of crust and core before you made it there. It was never supposed to see the light of day.

Moccus and Rudra were standing above Jackson. It has been three weeks and he has still not regained consciousness. They are humming loudly and producing a bright light around him. They stop. Rudra pushes Moccus' hands down and shakes his head. There is a sadness lingering in the air, but also an uneasiness. Xander could strike at any time and with Jackson and Victoria being so weak, they couldn't fight him.

The light from the sun fades. There is only darkness and silence, save for the candles in the hallway. A deafening silence that is disturbingly quiet. When they are alive, the whole castle is filled with color and life. The flowers in the garden are normally full and bursting with color.

Now, everything is gray and bleak, the flowers are wilting and dying. Everything is dry and lifeless, there is no hope for Victoria. Most of the soldiers from the village are diurnal. Most of them are going to bed when Queen Victoria wakes up. She spends most of her nights sitting in a chair, outside the door of Jackson's room. There is a green bubble encasing him, for his safety, and hers. He tosses and turns in his sleep. Occasionally, he screams or mumbles something. Most of the dialogue is about Xander, but sometimes he calls for his love.

Today he didn't move. He never mumbled, and he never screamed. It was weirdly silent. Moccus, Maya, and Rudra turn in for the night. They're sleeping in their beds. It's not a peaceful sleep because they are worried about their son and Xander could attack at any minute. Victoria sat in her chair. Her hair was in a messy bun, she had no makeup on. She was only wearing a nightgown, a robe, and fuzzy slippers. She held a handkerchief in her hand, which she blew her nose into violently between sobs. There is a faint whooshing noise. A candle blows out behind Victoria. She turns to look at a mirror in the hallway. Xander is in the mirror. His eye is red, and the other is covered by an eye patch. He has shaved his head and his fangs are out.

"Xander, you did all of this, you piece of shit," Victoria says, angrily.

"I brought you a peace offering, but you can't have it for free," Xander whispers.

He holds a vial with a red liquid, his hand sticks out from the mirror. She grabs it and inspects it.

"This is the antidote for the magic that is killing him," Xander hisses. Victoria grabs it before he can pull his hand back. He is pulled halfway out of the mirror.

"How do I know that this isn't going to kill him, or make him crazy?" Victoria whispers angrily at him.

"What choice do you have, Queenie? I'm going to need time to regain my strength before we continue this little rendezvous. You don't come looking for me and I'll leave you alone," Xander says.

He reaches out of the mirror to shake her hand.

"How can I trust you? All you've done is fuck up the one great thing I had going. I was lonely because you put us here. Then when I finally found what I had been searching for you took it away. True to form, you never fail to disappoint me, Isaac," Victoria says.

"Well, it's either this, or he'll die, and we have to start over anyway," Xander replies.

"I don't trust you and I'm not making any deals with you. You're a lying, manipulative, selfish piece of shit. You don't even care about Gabbi. How could you treat humans like that? Have I taught you nothing?" Victoria whispers and cries.

"I'm done with your lessons and your patronizing, I am one of the eight, we're equals," Xander hisses.

"Well, that's news to me. You act like you're above us, all of this. You were the one who manipulated me into stepping out on him in the first place. Then I tried to give you your powers back and how do you repay me? By trying to destroy everything. If he dies, I will blow everything up and start over. It's not time yet, if that happens right now there won't be a next time," Victoria says.

"I know, it will be time soon, trust me. That's why I'm giving you medicine for him," Xander says.

"Why are you not attacking, right now, while we're vulnerable? You could just take him out and I could blow us all up, what are you waiting for?" Victoria yells.

"Soon," Xander hisses ominously.

The mirror fills with red smoke, and he disappears. She stamps her feet, looks at the vial, and leaves the room. Victoria zooms to Jackson's side. She takes down the protective bubble and he wakes immediately. He clenches Victoria's throat. His eyes glow bright, white light. He chokes her unconscious. She loses her grip on the vial and drops it on the floor. Jackson drops her, hard, then picks up the bottle and opens the lid. He sips it. His eyes go back to how they normally look. He shakes his head and rubs the sleep out of his eyes.

He looks down and sees what he has done to Victoria. She isn't bleeding, but nor is she moving, and she has deep marks on her neck. He picks her up and holds her head in his arms. She is pale and lifeless. He holds her and rocks her in his arms. He cries, his tears rolling down his cheeks. They land on her face. The teardrops light up as they hit her face. She gasps for air, then she coughs. Jackson smiles and rubs her face with his hand. She looks up and smiles back at him.

"Jack," she coughs, "Is that really you? You're back."

Her voice is very hoarse.
"Don't talk, I'm so sorry Vic, I didn't mean to, I thought you were Xander," Jackson says.

He cries more, and holds her tight. Jackson stands up with a great effort. He is only wearing a robe and pajama pants. The bandage on his side is showing. He winces in pain as he gets up. Victoria helps him up. It is a struggle for her to stand too. A guard has seen everything.

He enters the room followed by Moccus, Maya, and Rudra. Rudra pushes his way in. He rushed to his son's aide, then Maya ran in after him to help Victoria. They support them to get onto the bed. Jackson and Victoria are sitting upright in the bed. Rudra grabs a nearby chair and sits right next to Jackson. Maya rubs Victoria's hand. She finds a chair and sits on the other side of the bed.

"Son, it's so good to see you. How are you doing? Are you really back?" Rudra asks excitedly.

"Yeah, Dad, I'm okay. Vic helped me come out of the cave," Jackson says.

"You weren't in the cave, son. You were here in bed, in a coma. Queenie never left your side. What did you think happened?" Rudra asks.

"I was in the cave. Xander and I were in a long battle. Every day he would visit me. He had me shackled to the wall and he would only unshackle me to fight. He would always win, but he would never let me die. He would just show me the atrocities that he inflicted on Vic. He would make me listen to her wailing over and over again. It never stopped. Then I choked him out and Vic was standing at the mouth of the cave. I just walked out, and all of a sudden she was right here on the floor," Jackson said.

"You were here the whole time. We worked on getting you out of there every day. It's been almost a month," Rudra explains.

"Dad, I would never have hurt Vic," Jackson says.

"I know, babe, you thought I was Xander. You kept telling me to let you go, then you choked me until I passed out." Victoria says with a raspy voice.

"Honey, don't talk, you're hurt. Let's get you some tea." Maya says, rubbing her hand.

Maya snaps her fingers. Wilson appears with a cup of tea and a napkin on a saucer. Maya gets up and places it on a desk in the corner of the room, near the bed. Then she points at Victoria, putting her in the chair by magic. Next Maya points at the desk, and the chair zooms into place there. Maya points again, and the napkin unfolds itself and places itself on her lap. Victoria picks up the teacup, nods, and takes a sip. There is a mob of soldiers forming in the doorway and there is a commotion happening.

"Moccus, can you take care of the rubberneckers?" Maya asks, not even looking at him.

"Yeah, I got it. Then I'm going back to bed. Call me when there's cake," he says with a heavy sigh.

Moccus leaves the room. Maya points at the door. It slams and locks. Maya and Rudra are hyper-focused on what Jackson is saying. Victoria is listening, but also enjoying her tea and massaging her throat.

"Son, you can't just go after him right now. He's counting on that. He'll finish the job and I'm not going to let that happen, not after how hard we fought to get you back," Rudra says forcefully.

"Dad, he's still out there. We're vulnerable. Why wouldn't he take the opportunity to strike now?" Jackson argues. Victoria clears her throat. They look at her.

"He's not coming after us yet. He told me," Victoria says, then coughs.

"How are you so sure, Queenie?" Rudra asks, skeptically.

"Why do you think Jackson is awake?" Maya chimes in.

Rudra turns to her.

"Well, what do you know? How come I'm the last one to know everything?" Rudra asks frustratedly.

"Queenie talked to him. He gave Jack the antidote," Maya answers, casually.

"How long, Maya?" Rudra asks, angrily.

"I've known she was going to make a deal with him for about a week," Maya says.

"And you didn't think you should share that with the rest of the class?" Rudra yells.

"I can't always tell people when I have a foreboding. Most of the time you brush me off anyway. Besides, sometimes I only know a little bit of what happens, it's not always clear," Maya says.

"Did he trick me or is it real?" Victoria asks, having trouble swallowing.

"It cured Jack. He didn't lie about that. But we're not done with him yet. He has a bigger plan," Maya says.

"Well, what is it?" Rudra asks.

"I don't know. I just know that this is the first part of his plan and he'll come back, and that's all I saw," Maya says.

"You're no help. Maybe I'll pull a Xander, just up and leave my partner. I don't want to be with someone that lies," Rudra yells.

Maya rolls her eyes, "You wouldn't make it a day without me. You'd call me crying because you'd have to suck your own dick," she yells back.

"Oh, my goddess, ma! Gross!" Jackson yells.

They stick their tongues out at each other.

"You can just figure out how to fig yourself then," Maya says.

"I'm going to kill myself. That's not an image I will ever get out of my brain now," Jackson says to himself as he shivers in disgust.

"Guys, can I just lie down? My throat is killing me," Victoria barely squeaks out.

"Right, I'm so sorry, Queenie. We should all get some rest," Maya says.

Rudra and Maya walk towards the door, still arguing.

"Well, there are a lot of rooms in this castle. You can just go find one and sleep by yourself, how about that?" Maya sneers.

"Maybe I will," Rudra retorts.

They exit and close the door behind them. You can still hear them arguing through the closed door.

"They'll be fine. Give them ten minutes and they'll go back to humping. This is foreplay for them, trust me. One of their biggest fights ended in them on their disgusting sex swing - don't ask," Jackson says.

They laugh, Victoria clutches her throat and they melt into each other's arms. Victoria lays in the bed with him, leaning her head on his shoulder. He smiles and kisses her. They lay down and for the first time in at least six hundred years, Victoria fell asleep during the night. They were together again, and nothing else mattered. At least for now, the sounds of their partner breathing finally brought them both peace. No more night terrors or uncontrollable wailing. It was quiet. It wasn't a solemn silence, it was peaceful for the first time in months.

The next morning, the ballroom was made up of many tables in rows. There was a stage set up and a special table set up on the stage. Wilson is hard at work setting the tables at the speed of light. There are balloons, streamers, and decorations everywhere. Gabbi is on her cellphone, recording herself for her social media followers. She sings off-key and tells her followers about the party she's going to. She says it's going to be a spectacular party that only she was invited to. She ends her livestream with her signature pose. Veera sees her and walks up to her.

"Hey, Gabbi, do you have a date for tonight?" Veera asks, shyly.

"No, normally I'm not allowed to date anyone who's not Master. Now that I'm not with Master, does the rule still count? Are you going to take me back to him?" Gabbi asks innocently, looking at Veera wide-eyed.

"Do I have a secret admirer?" Gabbi grabs her phone and records herself saying, "Hey fam, I just heard that I have a secret admirer and they're going to ask me to the dance tonight," Gabbi makes silly noises, then stops recording.

"Well, I kind of rescued you from your master. I was wondering if you would go with me?" Veera asks, hesitantly.

"Oh, my goddess, I'm so happy it's you! I thought it was Wilson. I mean he's cool or whatever, but he's so not my type. You're hot and rich. Hell yes, I'll go with you," Gabbi laughs.

"How old are you?" Veera asks.

"I'm thirty, in, like, human years. But now that I'm immortal, it's like cat years, right?" Gabbi asks.

"I'm not sure how all of that works. Come with me and we'll figure it out together," Veera says, holding his arm out.

She takes it and giggles. She jumps up and down and kisses him on the cheek. Veera blushes.

Later that night, the ballroom is packed to the brim with soldiers and guests of all types. Rudra, Maya, Jackson, Adam, and Victoria all sit at the table on the stage. Rudra clinks his wine glass with his fork. The room hushes. Everyone is dressed in their most formal attire. Victoria and Jackson looked rested and put together, even though both of them were still recovering.

Victoria was wearing a beautiful lavender dress, a matching hat, and fishnet gloves. She has a scarf around her neck to cover the damage left by Jackson's fugue state.

"This first toast goes to my wonderful son and one of my best friends. We have been through hell and back, but you two fought and helped all of us get through it. Cheers!" Rudra's voice booms and echoes through the ballroom.

"Cheers!" the crowd replies, and they all take a drink.

"Next, we need to give a special thank you to Wilson. This little guy has been a stable source of hope for all of us. Can you please come up here, buddy?" Rudra says he points at Wilson and signals him to come to the stage. Wilson zooms to the stage. Rudra picks him up and puts him on his shoulder. Maya presents him with a medal around his neck. She raises his hand in the air.

"Cheers!" the crowd says again, and they all drink. Rudra sets Wilson down gently and pats his head. The crowd hushes.

"On a sadder note, our fighting is not even close to being done. We have won a very big battle, but it is not over by a long shot. There will be another time that I will call on you and ask you to fight with me. Will you be there?" Rudra booms.

The crowd roars, "Yeah!"

The walls tremble by the force of the cheering. Rudra calms them again. They hush.

"Then let's enjoy the break. This is for all of you. I know I'm hungry. Let's feast!" Rudra booms.

The crowd cheers uncontrollably. A giant feast appears, filling every plate on all of the tables. The goblets refill as the crowd is feasting. A band on the stage plays jazz music. Victoria feels a strange breeze on her neck. She turns around, but there is no one behind her. Then she looks in the crowd and sees Xander's single red eye, glowing at a table towards the back. Victoria nods her head and raises her glass to him. He nods back and raises his glass to her.

"I'm not going anywhere, Mistress. You'll never get rid of me," Xander whispers in her mind.

"I'm counting on it," Victoria replies.

"I will always be here, in the shadows, watching you, waiting for my moment to strike. I'll come back for my payment soon. By the way, you look beautiful tonight," Xander says in her mind.

"Cheers," she thinks.

She takes a sip of her goblet. The red wine drips down her lips and lands on her dress. She looks down to clean it with a napkin, then looks up. Xander was gone. But the connection she had forged with him, in blood, was never going away. She could kill his essence, but it would just come back like some kind of roach. Disgusting sewer-dwelling bugs could survive a nuclear blast. That is the description of a cockroach. Whatever Xander was, he was a persistent pest. Victoria made a choice a long time ago to have three people in her life. Now she had to mend the bond that she had broken, or this struggle would never end.

The laws of the universe were in order for now. How long before this shaky house of cards comes crumbling down? Victoria didn't care. All she could think about was having her warm monkey man next to her. She knew everything would be ok.

The party ended several hours later. The sun was about to start peaking over the mountains. Jackson carried Victoria and flew to the top of the castle roof. They danced in the twilight.

He dipped her and they kissed as the sun rose slowly in the sky. He picked her up and took her to their room. They got ready for bed. They laid down, got under the covers, and Victoria laid her head on his arm. She just stared into his eyes and drank him in. Nothing could ruin this, not even Xander. She sits up and looks in the mirror. She sees Xander staring, hiding in the shadows. His reflection laughs a sinister laugh. All he can do now is wait, fast and think.

Victoria gasps, "He'll never leave me alone."

To Be Continued

Milton Keynes UK
Ingram Content Group UK Ltd.
UKHW020640120824
446671UK00001B/11